THE TENT

& Other Stories

By

Caroline Arlen

Also by Caroline Arlen:
Colorado Mining Stories; Hazards, Heroics &
Humor

For Lars

TABLE OF CONTENTS

THE TENT

The ground was hard and cold, the air so frigid the stars seemed frozen into the blackness. I could hear desert creatures around me—wild mustangs snorting, prairie dogs rustling through the brittle grass—but the only thing I could see was my white breath, drifting away.

With chill-stiffened joints, I began to set up camp. I attached a can of butane to my MSR backpacker stove. I had bought it while in college in Vermont, when I fancied myself an outdoorsy woman. After graduation, I left that part of my life behind and moved to New York City to be a journalist. I met my future husband there, and we relocated to Washington, D.C., so he could save the children. He played golf with senators while I landed within an inner circle of wives who discussed what type of dress or suit was appropriate at which social events. I also spent a good deal of time at the dentist from grinding my teeth so hard they fractured.

This article assignment for *U.S. News* about a wild horse roundup was my first freelance job since moving to southwest Colorado. It wasn't until I had driven through Dove Creek that night and turned off onto the dark desert road that I considered what it would mean if it turned out I no longer had the skills to be a reporter, what that would mean for my ability to make a living; even more, what it would say about my decision to leave my husband, along with our parquet wood floors and marble fireplaces.

I turned on the butane and it hissed through the hose to the stove. I flicked my lighter. Nothing. I turned up the gas and flicked the lighter again. *Poof!* Blue flames whirled out across the ground in an inverse mushroom shape. I jumped up and stomped out the spot fires. Then I decided to look at the instructions and turned the stove right side up.

I heated a small pot of water until it boiled, then dumped in a baggie, awakening from the dead a ten-year-old package of freeze-dried black bean chili. The steam thawed my nose enough that I noticed the smells around me, sage—clay sand, and sweet, acidic horse manure. I filled my lungs with the scent of manure.

I had always believed I loved horses because of the way they moved, their power and coordination. But now what first came to mind when I thought of horses was the image of them sleeping standing up, at peace yet ready to run.

As a child, I used to sleep in absurd positions, legs up the wall, head drooping off the edge of the bed. I did this under the guise of being funny. I liked the idea of my parents coming in to wake me in the morning and finding me looking like I'd been in a train wreck. Maybe this had also been my way of booby-trapping myself so that if a crack in the earth started to open and swallow me, I would fall over and wake up.

Don, from the Bureau of Land Management, had said the wild horse roundup would take place at dawn. He told me that everyone involved was going to camp out near the site. But I didn't see any other cars when I arrived. I considered that I might be in the wrong place, but it was late. I was on a BLM road, miles from any traffic, so I decided to stay put and get some rest.

I pulled my old crescent-shaped "Eureka!" tent out of its stuff sack. The gray nylon was so stiff from disuse that even though I followed the instructions this time, my efforts at tugging the rods through the loops bent some of them into distortion. The tent wound up looking like a crippled bug.

I licked my index finger and held it up to feel for wind direction. The air current was so faint I had to wet my finger again. I felt a slight cooling on the right side of my cuticle and rotated my tent's domed back toward the almost nonexistent breeze.

When I crawled into it with my sleeping bag, I tried to zip up the door flap, but the opening was too stretched for it to close more than halfway. I lay back on my mat and started to worry about snakes, the rattlesnakes Don warned me about, slithering in through the door gap. So I focused on the stars I could see through the opening. They captivated me the way a campfire usually would, but without the comforting warmth. I pulled the sleeping bag over my head.

I thought I'd been looking at the stars, but I was really staring at what was between them. The void. That's what called to me. And that's what scared me.

I had once loved my husband very much, the boyish wisp of hair dusting his determined eyes. Over time, I became mostly enthralled by his ability to move through life with such beauty and confidence. While I was concentrating on trying to be the right companion to this seemingly perfect creature, I disappeared.

I got it right sometimes, the wife thing, but sometimes I got it very wrong. I had worn the correct all-purpose black velvet dress, but with open-toed shoes, in the fall! I had known all the right things to say: "Have you lost weight?" "What do you do?" "Oh my, that sounds fascinating." But every now and then, with my fuses fizzled on chardonnay, I launched into one of my funny stories, to an ambassador's wife, who was already glaring at my shoes. Maybe it was the story about the time I got trapped in a port-o-john at an endurance horse race. Or the one about getting thrown off my horse in Central Park and landing, doggy-style, on a jogging doctor. I would suddenly become aware of the sound of my laughter, because it was so isolated and singular.

At first light, I crawled out of the tent and pulled on my boots. I turned on my car and hunched over the steering wheel, rubbing my arms while I waited for the engine to warm. When hot air came out of the vents, I held my frozen tube of toothpaste up to one of them. I got out and paced around to get my circulation going. I brushed my teeth and then spat the blue froth into the dust. While I pushed dirt over it with my boot, I heard a distant rumbling.

I jogged up the small hill between the road and my camp and watched an approaching convoy of pickup trucks, horse trailers, and flatbed trucks. I got into my car and tagged on to the end of the procession. Red clay dust sifted in through the vents, caking the black dashboard. Although my hands still shook from the cold, I managed to turn the radio from NPR to a country music station to better match the setting.

The convoy stopped where the road turned into sand dunes. Six men unloaded metal bars and poles off the flatbeds. While they assembled a couple of corrals, I wandered the grounds, trying to shake the chill out of my legs.

"You must be the reporter," a man said behind me.

I turned to him, moving my gaze upward until it stopped at his tan cowboy hat.

Don wore a canvas jacket over a light blue shirt with snaps. He removed his baseball cap and wiped his bangs with his forearm. We shook hands. He sipped his coffee, sucking the remnant caffeine from his brown mustache.

He waved his cap toward a red clay canyon wall. "That's where we're gonna put ya. Horses will come in through that end." His green eyes were surrounded by hardened skin that wrinkled when he squinted into the sunlight. "Hey, Bob!" he yelled toward the corrals. "Don't close the dang gates yet! We gotta get 'em in there first." He laughed and shook his head, then looked at the ground. He smoothed the dirt with the toe of his boot. "Okay, let's go," he said, and walked away.

As Don continued up the canyon wall, his hips swiveled as he walked, his gait truncated by his tight Wrangler jeans.

The trail narrowed where it traversed the side of a 200-foot drop. As I crossed it, my vision gave way to spots of light. I tried to focus on the faded ring of Don's tobacco tin embedded in his back pocket, but my fear of heights took over. My legs became spongy and gave way. I lowered myself until I could touch the hard ground.

I felt a hand on my arm and tried to focus my eyes. Don sat beside me on the rim and asked, "Are you okay?"

"I'm sorry," I muttered. "I'm afraid of heights."

"Let's take a breather," he said, exhaling long and slow, as if to show me how. I leaned back against the rock wall.

I wasn't so much afraid of heights as I was of edges. When I was near a cliff edge, I imagined myself tripping and falling. I once learned in Driver's Education that staring at a hazard might cause you to steer toward it. The same was true with kayaking: if you're heading toward a rock in the river and fixate on that rock, even for the sake of avoiding it, you're in much more danger of hitting it than if you didn't even know it was there. I was so afraid of making a misstep and falling, I believed that fear made me predisposed to doing just that. It was an inevitability. So, a voice inside me would say, *Oh, just jump and get it over with.* That's what I was afraid of; that I would just get it over with.

Don stood, helped me up, and didn't let go of my hand. When I resisted his grasp, he said, "It's okay. You're all right." I followed him. Then, trying to regain some semblance of professionalism, I let go of his hand and trudged past him toward the top of the ridge.

Once we were at the lookout position, Don said he was going to radio below for an update on the helicopter. "All right," he said into the walkie-talkie. "We'll be on the lookout for them."

On the horizon, beyond the canyon, a dust cloud was building. A fly-sized helicopter emerged. It rocked from side to side around the dust cloud. It became larger and louder. Don passed me his binoculars. "You should be able to see Spot now, the pinto stallion."

Horse heads hammered out, then back, into the approaching dust, manes wild. Legs churned. A small colt, sandwiched between two mares, stumbled, then regained his footing. Spot surged out in front. He was white, with large black markings in the shape of puzzle pieces. He was not very big for a stallion, but he looked fierce with his head held aloft and nostrils flared.

"He's magnificent," I said, and lowered the glasses.

Don crossed his arms over his puffed-up chest and grinned. Then his arms dropped and he grabbed the binoculars from me. "What the hell?" he said. The radio crackled and he picked it up. "No, I don't know what's going on. They were goin' good. Then they just split."

The mustangs had divided, veering off in two different directions: one group toward the mouth of the canyon, as planned; the other, led by Spot, toward the canyon rim across from us.

"Okay, here's what we do," Don said into the radio. "Let the Judas horse make his run to bring in the first bunch, and get the chopper to go after the stray pack."

A man on a palomino led another horse out of the corral area. The cowboy arched backward as he pulled the swaybacked horse, trotting up the bottom of the canyon. Don said, "We call it the Judas horse because we take a domesticated horse and set it loose in front of the stampeding wild herd. All it wants to do is not get run over and go back to the corral where there's free food. The wild pack gets tricked into following him into captivity."

The cowboy, on his palomino, and the Judas horse stood behind an outcropping and waited. When the mustangs got closer, the cowboy removed the swayback's halter and slapped him on the hind end.

I knew that some of the captured mustangs would be looked at by a vet and released. Some would be auctioned off to good families or ranches, as a way of culling the herd. The grass on BLM land could only support a certain number of horses without the risk of starvation. But, inevitably, some of the mustangs would wind up in the hands of people who then sold them to glue factories for a profit.

The old Judas horse galumphed through the canyon beneath us. He was probably a retired pack horse or an old trail horse from a dude ranch. He certainly didn't know he was caught up in a Greek tragedy. But I wondered why the mustangs couldn't recognize that he was not one of them, that following him was a bad idea.

I wanted to run into the canyon, to stop the wild horses. Did I love horses that much? Maybe. But what I was really thinking was, *How had I let my life get away from me? How had I let myself get swallowed up? When did I stop sleeping with my legs up the wall?*

The chopper bobbed and circled around the other band of horses, trying to wrangle them toward the mouth of the canyon. But the mustangs, commanded by Spot, spun and pranced along the cliff in front of the whirring, thumping helicopter blades.

"What a mess!" Don shifted his weight side to side. "What made them split like that?" he shouted into the walkie-talkie as he scanned the area with his binoculars. "Damn!" He stopped moving. "There's a goddamn tent out there! Yeah, that's what did it. Who the hell... Well, I don't know either."

I felt my head grow faint. I turned to Don, my eyes wide. "A tent?"

"Yeah, look." He handed me the glasses.

I leveled them on my pathetic excuse for a tent, which was now covered in dust and looking shell-shocked. "Yup," I said, handing him back the binoculars. "Looks like a tent. Wow."

Spot's band was cornered on a precipice. The chopper swung back and forth to cover the escape routes into the desert. Their only clear pathway was into the canyon, toward the corrals, but they weren't going. Instead, Spot stomped out toward the helicopter, arched his neck, and pawed the dirt.

"I don't believe this!" Don said into the radio. "Make sure our pilot doesn't think he's back in 'Nam and try to engage our stallion." Don bowed his head and rubbed his brow. "Damn it!" he said, stomping his foot. "I finally get a reporter out here and this happens."

I took in a deep breath and exhaled. I turned my back to the roundup: the mustangs, the Judas horse, the corrals, my ill-fated attempt at camping; then spun around again and stuffed my hands into my back pockets. "Don," I said. "That's my tent."

He looked at me. "You're joking."

I squinted at the mustangs on the other side of the canyon. Spot pranced out a few steps, reared up, and thrashed at the whirling dust.

"What were you thinking?"

I shook my head and shrugged. *That's it,* I thought. *I've blown it. Maybe I'm not meant to be a reporter, or out here, or any of it.* Spot trotted back toward his herd. The mares turned in circles.

Don laughed. "You must have froze! We packed up and went to a hotel." He stared at me, snorted, then shook his head. "Way to tough it out!"

Spot stopped. He took a few side-to-side steps, then turned and charged the helicopter at a dead run. I gasped and pointed.

Don smashed the walkie-talkie against his cheek. "Ed! Up! Get the chopper to back off! Pull up!" Then he glanced over at me. "We got what we need."

As soon as the chopper began to lift, Spot stormed out beneath it, throwing his head about. The herd followed, running and bucking. Their manes whipped behind them as they returned out into the desert.

Don heaved a sigh, winked at me, and said, "I think you've got yourself a pretty good story. You like that ending?"

I laughed and nodded. "Yeah."

As we walked back down, Don stopped at the exposed 200-foot drop. He offered his hand. "No, I'm okay," I said, preoccupied with the image of Spot fighting the helicopter and how to work it into my article. I studied the horses in the corral beneath me, where the cowboys paired mares with their foals. Halfway down, I set up my tripod.

After I took a few rolls of photographs, I drove back to my campsite and got out. Although the tent was a little worse for wear, it still stood. Only one corner had been ripped off its stake, leaving the cover fly to blow around in the wind. Every time the fly rose and splayed out, that little broken bug of a tent screamed, "Eureka!" Then it fluttered down again. Then up, white strings straight out—Eureka! It had probably been celebrating itself for hours.

POSSE

A slant of late afternoon sunlight glanced off the Animas River. The autumnal current was shallow and swift. My cheeks bristled in the crisp air as I raised my new fishing rod and drew it back. I steadied my feet on the rocky bank and cast the line. My plastic minnow lure from Woolworth's sailed through the air. One of the reasons I had chosen Durango, over other southwestern towns, was because it had a Woolworth's downtown, as well as a Coast-to-Coast Hardware store, not just touristy T-shirt shops and window displays of Native American jewelry.

The fishing line tightened, and I pulled back, yanking up an algae-bedraggled twig. I reeled it in, pulled off the slimy detritus, and re-cast the lure, this time toward a darkened eddy pool downstream from the bridge's center pylon. A truck pulling a horse trailer crossed over in the direction of Missionary Ridge. A mud-caked Subaru, stacked with kayaks, drove the other way toward City Market, where some people would be shopping for their supper.

I liked this version of myself: fishing for my food. Old school. There was really no other reason—other than projecting this new idea of me—for me to be down at the riverbank, with my tin bucket for my prospective dinner. Just a hundred feet up the road, City Market was having a sale on Van de Kamp fish sticks. But I hadn't moved to Colorado to wander fluorescent grocery aisles in search of fish sticks. No, this was a better western look for me, replete with Wrangler jeans and an orange hunting jacket because it was hunting season. Though probably not at the 32nd Street bridge.

The line tightened again. I reeled in a small, speckled fish and lifted it from the cold water of the Animas, Rio de Las Animas Perdidas, the river of lost souls. The trout's gills panted. I stuck my fingers under its jaw and snapped its head back.

I took my "kill" home, driving up the dirt road into our neighborhood of warped, weathered duplexes. I had moved into my house late that summer, then had almost immediately been called away on a freelance magazine assignment.

My neighbors sat at the top of the porch steps. I had spoken with Fran and Lilly only a few times. Fran, the taller and more imposing of the two women, peered in the bucket. "Did you catch that in the Animas?"

"I did!"

Fran looked up at me. Her thick gray hair was pulled back in a ponytail. "We generally don't eat the fish. We do catch and release around here."

My jaw tightened. "Well, that's nice, but what if you're hungry?"

"Oh, it's not for ethical reasons," Lilly said. She had a porcelain complexion with patches of rosacea on her cheeks. "We don't eat the fish because of contamination from the mines up in Silverton."

I looked down at my little fish, half expecting to see three eyeballs.

Once inside, I rummaged through my unpacked moving boxes for something I could use to dig a hole. Fran and Lilly had left by the time I brought my bucket down the porch steps. It took several attempts to get my new Wranglers to bend at the knees before I was able to kneel on the ground. I dug my clipboard into the arid dirt, breathing in the wafting dust tinged with sagebrush.

Lilly came out on the deck. She dunked a teabag up and down in her steaming mug. "We have a shovel you could borrow," she said.

"Thanks, but I think I've got it." The hole was already three inches deep.

By now, I had concluded that Fran and Lilly were "together." I suppose when I moved from the East Coast to the land of rodeos and white-water rafting, I didn't expect my first neighbors to be a couple of mild-mannered lesbians, but I had not thought long enough on the subject for it to register a feeling.

I lay the fish down in the hole and straightened its head.

Lilly blew on her tea. "Why are you burying the fish?" she asked.

"Well, I'm not going to eat the poor polluted thing."

"Yes, but why are you burying it? It's a fish."

I shrugged. "I feel bad." I pushed what I had dug over the silvery fish and patted it down.

"I thought you said you were from New York."

When the doorbell rang the next morning, it was Harvey, the plumber. He said, "Gotta crawl under your house, ma'am. Landlord wants me to replace the freeze valve before winter."

Harvey looked in the mudroom. It was cluttered with mud boots, cross-country skis, and old wooden snowshoes from my college years in Vermont. Harvey gathered up the stuff and dumped it out on the living room floor. "Previous tenants always leave behind a bunch of crap," he said.

"That's my crap," I mumbled.

Harvey was short and stocky, but kind of flattened, as if he came from a clan genetically adapted to crawl spaces. "Okay," he said. Then he snapped his red suspenders and disappeared through the trap door. After clanking around for a while, he climbed out. "I tell ya, with so many outsiders swarming into Durango, developers are just throwing up these garbage pails for buildings."

"I'm sorry," I said.

"Why? You didn't build it."

"I mean, for moving here." I had noticed that newcomers didn't seem very welcome, which is why I was trying to blend in.

As Harvey wrote up the receipt, he said, "You just get divorced?"

I nodded. "What makes you say that?"

"Those eight-foot-tall skis look like they've been pulled out of storage from a bygone era." He handed me the receipt. "Hey, there's a bar downtown called Farquahrts. They have a live band every Friday for Happy Hour. Everyone goes. You should go."

I stared at the clump of rotted dirt stuck to his top lip and wondered if he might be asking me out on a date, but Harvey just turned and walked out.

I started to close the door behind him, but it bumped into a silver-toed boot. I let the door swing back open. Attached to the boot was a man with curly black hair and graying sideburns. He grinned. "Hi! My name is Robert, but I go by Dr. Rob. I'm a chiropractor."

The doctor wore a cropped, scoop-neck T-shirt. Gold chains lay across his hairy chest. He crossed his arms. "I watched you move in a couple of months ago, but I figured I'd wait for a better time to introduce myself."

"Is this a better time for you?"

"Yeah, I live over there." He pointed to the duplex across the dirt road from mine. "I own my own chiropractic business." Dr. Rob reached up to place a hairy-knuckled hand on the doorframe above my head. "My psychic predicted that you'd be coming." He emitted a sputtering laugh, then wiped his mustache. "You're a Gemini, aren't you?"

"No, a journalist." I started to close the door.

He furrowed his brow, then shrugged.
"Well, I'm also kind of new here.

I was wondering if you might want to go to Farquahrts sometime."

"I'm sorry, I have to unpack," I said, and shut the door, successfully this time.

Most afternoons I went down to where the Animas River passed through Durango, then banked around Santa Rita Park's two soccer fields. At the heart of the park was Smelter, a Class IV rapid, as well as a water treatment plant.

I sat on the bank above the rapid and sketched kayakers surfing the conflagrating current. The sewage stench was no longer noticeable now that the hot summer months had passed. The kayakers would nose into the whitewater waves and get spit out and spun around like bull riders. The boaters would scatter to either side of the rapid to make way for commercial rafts, which occasionally flipped in the massive center hole, scattering shrieking tourists into the tumult.

Amid all the commotion and chatter between the kayakers and their friends on the banks, I felt like I was being social, that I had pals and was part of something. As the sun began to set, so did the mirage of my social life. I then drove to Romero's for chili rellenos. By insinuating myself into its bustling atmosphere, and deploying and scribbling notes in my writing pad, I could again feel like I was with people and yet also very busy, so very, very busy doing something important.

These nibbles of a social life carried me for a while, but as the days shrank, so did my mood and self-confidence. I began to long for actual human contact and conversation, someone to take even a vague interest in me. I concluded it was time to brave Happy Hour at Farquahrts.

That Friday, I wove my long blond hair into a French braid. I pulled on a pair of Lucky jeans and put on some rouge. After parking my black Suzuki Sidekick on a side street, I strode down Main Street toward The

Farquahrts Saloon. Electric guitar riffs reverberated out onto the sidewalk.

When I neared the picture-glass window showcasing the bar's rock 'n' roll band, I sped up, walked past the open door, and continued around the block. On the next pass, I slowed just enough to glance into the doorway packed with shoulder-slapping locals. Beyond them, inside, were steps and a narrow balcony lined with people on either side, gauntlet-style. Again, I sped up and slingshot around the block.

On the third pass, I lowered my head and dove through the pod of people in the entrance, then sidestepped through the gauntlet. The bar counter was three people deep, with mostly men holding sloshing pitchers of beer. I breached the male wall to gain access to one of the bartenders. I raised my gaze from the floor to order a tequila shot and a Rolling Rock. The dance floor was packed, the music infectious. It wasn't long before I was swing dancing to the Rolling Stones with the City Planner. I had done it...something, though I wasn't sure what.

Most mornings I passed Kat, Dr. Rob's duplex neighbor, on our way to and from the mailboxes at the bottom of our dirt road. She was small and sturdy, with a determined walk and the stern focus of a baseball pitcher. I had first noticed Kat when she closed her hand in her car door and let loose a litany of very specific and shocking curse words. I was surprised to later learn she was a kindergarten teacher.

We rarely spoke, but the morning after my Farquahrts pilgrimage she greeted me with crossed arms at the mailboxes. "Saw you at Happy Hour. Those guys were all over you like fresh meat."

"What?"

"Seriously!" Kat had freckles and a ponytail geyser of red hair erupting from the top of her head. "There are so many more men than women in Durango, it can be a little overwhelming. Especially when winter nears and the bucks start rutting for a warm body to bed down with."

I cleared my throat. "Funny. I thought we were dancing."

Kat laughed. "You were."

When my phone rang a few days later, I thought it would be my landlord calling for my past-due December rent, but it was Justin.

"Who?" I asked.

"I'm the guy who was standing by the rail at the bar...black T-shirt? Cowboy hat?"

Although we hadn't met, I did remember him. He was tall, with a tanned complexion and pale blue eyes. He said that the City Planner had told him who I was. Had I given Sam my last name? Well, it didn't matter.

We went to Trimble Hot Springs. Justin looked kind of funny wet, large, tanned arms hanging off a pale torso. White legs. He talked about his horses and packing into the Weminuche Wilderness. His stubble glistened. The darkness around him steamed. I dipped my head back into the hot water.

Dr. Rob rang my doorbell the next morning. He wore a T-shirt cut just above his hairy navel. "I saw that cowboy drop you off," he said. "You're better than that. Did I tell you I own my own business?" He winked and put his hands on his hips.

I closed the door.

I was on the porch with Fran and Lilly when Justin came to pick me up on his Harley. "I didn't know you have a motorcycle," I said.

Oh, yes, he was all man.

We rumbled off down a county road to a dingy bar called The Billy Goat. While I inspected the pool cues, Justin fetched us a couple of tequila shots. I racked the pool balls.

Justin broke, then walked around the table. He leaned forward and sank a striped ball. "You know, you should be careful who you hang out with."

I banked the two ball, but it missed the pocket. "What do you mean?"

"Those ladies next door to you. You might not have known it, but they're gay." He struck the cue ball so hard it hopped off the table and rolled across the wood floor. He went to fetch it and then placed it back down on the green felt. "Just thought I'd warn you. This is the West. Traditional values and all." He patted my cheek. "I'll get us another round."

When we left the bar, a snow flurry danced through the crisp night air. It was my first winter in eleven years outside a city full of sooty snow. My heart met the lightness of it. As we sped off on his Harley, I buried my face into the back of his leather jacket and felt protected. When Justin pulled into my driveway, I invited him in for Hot Pockets.

In the early morning, as I lay with my head in the depression beneath Justin's shoulder, someone knocked on my front door. I got up and went to the window. Dr. Rob stood in the thickly falling snow, looking up at my bedroom. He pounded on the door.

"Shit," Justin said, putting on his pants. "It's probably my wife."

Dr. Rob pounded on the door again.

"Your wife?!"

Dr. Rob kicked in the door.

Justin pulled on his shirt and grabbed his boots.

I went to the top of the stairs. "Get out!" I screamed at Dr. Rob. I then turned to Justin. "You too!"

By the time my headache dissipated enough for me to go outside, Fran and Lilly had cleared the snow from our deck. I walked tentatively across the slick boards.

Fran leaned on her shovel. "Just so you know, you'll be wanting to clear the snow off your side of the porch. We're happy to help, but just so you know."

"Yeah, just so you know," Lilly added. Her blue eyeliner ran down her pink cheeks. Lilly stuck her shovel into the bank, barely impacting it, and tossed off a little snow.

"Of course," I said. "I know that. I just got a late start this morning."

"We heard," Fran said.

I drove to town to buy a snow shovel. I got two, because I didn't know which one was better.

That afternoon, only a dusting of snow fell through the clouded sunshine. But by noon it started to come down thick again, unrelenting. After about a foot accumulated, I met Fran and Lilly on the porch to begin what would become a shoveling ritual. Every now and then the accumulation on the roof cascaded onto the porch, compounding our situation.

Across the road, Kat shoveled hers and Dr. Rob's porch. As each deluge from the roofs fell onto the porches, the snow packed against our windows, against the porch rails, and weighed heavy on the two-by-fours holding up our decks.

Despite all our shoveling, the roof kept letting go avalanches of snow. The porch snowpack rose to our waists and then above. We couldn't stay ahead of it. Lilly dropped her shovel. "I'm going to make some calls."

"I'm going to have to take a break too," I told Fran. "I've got a date."

"A date? In this?"

"Hey, you've got somebody to hibernate with. I don't."

"Make sure he can shovel."

Dan showed up wearing shorts over waffled long underwear. He used his jean jacket sleeve to scrape away the coating of ice on his Jeep's windshield. He laughed. "Defroster's broken."

We went to a pub. When he ordered his burger, he added, "And totally cook the shit out of it, dude." He leaned his head back. He was blond, with a chiseled, handsome face despite a crooked nose that looked like it had been broken at least once. He blinked slowly. "So, you're a writer." He seemed to be studying me, curious and interested. Then he said, "You should totally write about me." I wanted to go home. But he wanted to talk about his rich, mean parents in Vail, and how hard it was being a ski racer because chicks want a man with a real job.

By the time we left the pub, the snow had so blanketed Main Street, it was difficult to discern what was road and what was sidewalk. Dan's windshield wiper didn't work, so we tied my scarf to the blade. I asked him to let me out at the bottom of the road. I didn't want to spend the rest of the night pushing him out of a drift.

As I walked up the hill, a truck backed out of Kat's duplex. She stood in the doorway. The headlights passed over her red, tousled hair. When Kat saw me trudging up the road, she waved. "Wait!" she yelled, then went inside. She reemerged in a puffy orange ski suit.

We went to her carport and dragged out an old Finnish sled her grandfather had made. It was basically a straight-backed chair on two long runners, designed for one person to sit and another to push the sled, then stand and coast on the rails. Because Kat was so small, I did the pushing and coasting. The moon was full. We sailed down Main Street.

And the snow kept falling.

While we called for snowplows who wouldn't come.

While we slept.

In the morning, while Fran, Lilly, and I shoveled, Dr. Rob shuffled and skidded across the snow-packed road in his silver-tipped cowboy boots. He tried to walk up the steps to our porch but spun out and wound up facing the wrong direction. He turned back to face us. "How are you? You okay?"

"We're fine," Fran said. Lilly laughed.

"I wasn't talking to you." He wiped his nose and frosted mustache with his mitten. "I'm heading down to Phoenix. You should come with me."

"Me? Why?" I asked.

"Now's not the time to be headstrong. I can take care of you."

Fran snorted.

Dr. Rob sneered. "Oh, don't you roll your eyes at me, Fran. Some of us still believe in old-fashioned chivalry!"

I looked across at Kat shoveling their porch. "What about your house?"

He sniffed. "It's a rental. So what if I lose my damage deposit?"

"If your side of the porch goes, so will Kat's," I said.

"I told Kat she should come with me too. I can take care of you both." The cold was turning his nose a purplish shade of pale.

I scooped up a shovel of snow and flipped it on top of him. Dr. Rob slogged off and, soon after, drove away.

That afternoon, Dan's jeep turned up our drive, but his bald tires spun in the snow. He honked the horn, then got out. "Chair 8 is open at Purg! Let's go catch some powder!"

I stood up from my hunched shoveling stance and stretched backward. "I can't!" I yelled. "My porch is collapsing!"

He jutted his head back. "Dude! That's serious!" He put his hands on his hips. "Well, I'll catch ya later!"

Across the gully, Kat laughed. "Where are all our suitors now?!"

And the snow kept falling.

And falling.

Lilly came down with a cold. Fran and I struggled to keep up with the snow sliding off the roof onto our precariously propped-up porch. I watched as Kat set up a ladder on the side of her house. When she began to climb it, I yelled, "What the hell are you doing?"

"It's breaking in my roof!" Once on top, she started using a broom to push the snowpack past the rain gutters that were hindering its progression.

I took one of my shovels and slogged over to Kat's house. I climbed the ladder and tossed my shovel up ahead of me onto the slanted snowpack.

After a while, we took a break and reclined back on the roof, surrounded by darkness and stars. A blanket of night, touching warmth. I took in a deep breath, then sat up. As I stood, I slipped, fell backward, and slid on my butt toward the gutter. I tried to dig in my heels, but I went over the edge, taking a cascade of snow with me. I landed on the porch snow with an embedding crunch.

"Oh my God! Are you okay?" Kat yelled down.

I waved. "Peachy."

She laughed. "Well, catch ya later! No, wait!" She got to her knees. "This calls for rum!"

The next evening, while I read *The Hot Zone*, a thick mass of snow cascaded off the roof, burying the living room windows on the side of the house. The creaking porch began to whine. I opened my door. Fran was already approaching. She said, "I think we're in trouble."

We shoveled through the night, the wind chilling my sweat-dampened brow. Still, our building kept groaning like a wounded animal. Our efforts began to seem absurd. I sat down in the snow.

"Don't give up yet," Fran said, panting. She went into her house. A few minutes later, she returned with two steaming mugs.

"Tea? That's your solution?" I asked.

"It'll keep you going," she said and then slurped. "While we wait."

"For what?"

Fran smiled at me, then winked.

I squinted my eyes. "You know I'm not gay, right?"

She laughed. "Oh my God! Please tell me you didn't just say that."

"I'm sorry. I haven't been really good at reading people lately."

A truck, heading up our road, skidded out on the wet snow. It then backed up for another try. "They're here," Fran said.

"Who?"

The silver Ford-150 revved its engine and barreled up the drive, spinning up to our duplex.

"Our knights in shining armor," Fran said.

The Ford parked in the middle of the road. Four women piled out of the cab, each with a snow shovel. They lifted the tarp on the truck bed to reveal a beautiful, red Honda snowblower.

Lilly ran out in her robe and slippers and fell to her knees in the sea of white. "Jennie! Steph!" she cried out. A pink tissue was stuck to the tip of her nose. "You came! Ann? Kathy? You're our heroes!"

The driver, clad in Carhartt work pants and a cap pulled down over her forest of auburn hair, thrust a fist in the air. "Lesbian posse to the rescue!"

Eventually, though it was still snowing, the porch stopped creaking. We moved our efforts to Kat's porch. Kat, in her orange ski suit, brought out a thermos of rum cider and a stack of plastic cups. She plugged in a boom box and started shaking her hips and shoveling to her mixtape.

Some of us followed Kat's lead, dancing in a sort of stupor of fatigue, relief, and rum. When Jimmy Buffett started singing *Margaritaville*, all of us chimed in on the chorus while we shoveled. Fran grinned at me. "And they say chivalry is dead!" she shouted over the roar of the Honda blower, spewing its funnel of snow, flakes breaking off and falling like white confetti.

By the time I made it back to my house, I was so overheated, I stripped down to my Woolworths long underwear. I went to the kitchen and took a TV dinner out of the freezer. As I listened to the microwave whir, I saw my reflection in the window. I noticed that in addition to white long underwear, I was still wearing a wool hat with earflaps. I laughed and thought, *What a catch.*

SELF SUPPORT

A week after Labor Day, three men robbed a convenience store outside Cortez and fled in a stolen water truck. Before news of the robbery went out over the police radio, Colorado state patrolmen clocked the truck traveling over the speed limit and pursued it with flashing lights.

The robber driving the water truck decided to just pull over. Nobody knows why. The patrolmen soon realized they'd stopped the Cortez thieves' getaway vehicle. They drew their weapons; however, the robbers had semiautomatic rifles and strafed the police car. One of the officers survived and was able to call it in. Thus began an extensive, nationally broadcast manhunt. The three men, dressed in camouflage gear, were last seen running into the desert.

My friend Catherine and I had spent the last month planning a trip on the Dolores River, which snaked through that same desert. I had just moved to Durango and did not yet have a TV. Catherine didn't believe in them. So we did not know any details about the Cortez incident.

The night before our departure, I was playing pool at the Wildhorse Saloon with another friend, Mark. When I mentioned the trip, Mark raised his eyebrows. "Oh really? I heard the feds were shutting that down for the manhunt."

I debated passing on this information to Catherine, but I was so looking forward to this trip with her. In my mind, Catherine was a river-running goddess, with her sun-bleached hair, naturally deep-toned Italian complexion, and her reputation for having kayaked the Grand Canyon many times.

On the opposite side of the scale, I was still going to the community pool to learn how to roll my kayak back up after a flip. I had a "good roll" when practicing. But when it came to unplanned flips, like in a river, I had a particularly lousy roll, mostly because I never failed to yelp just before going under and would thus not have any air in my lungs to set up for a roll. So I'd inevitably wind up yanking my spray skirt off the cockpit and swimming the rapid.

In fact, I had no idea why Catherine invited a fledgling boater like me, except that maybe she wanted to show me the elegant but stark canyon of the river she loved. So I kept the information about the manhunt to myself. I figured the rangers would stop us if necessary.

Most river trips involve a group of people and begin with a lot of hustle and bustle. When running the Dolores, the boaters usually camp out the night before at the Pump House Station in order to get an early start on inflating the support rafts. Then they load the food, the fold-up tables, stoves, and the booze, as well as everyone's tents, sleeping bags, and dry bags filled with clothes and toiletries (meaning toothpaste and bug spray).

After pushing the support rafts off the bank to slop into the water, the kayakers begin to gear up. They drag their boats to the river's edge, tug on their wetsuits, spray skirts, PFDs, and helmets. Then they squeeze themselves into their cramped boats, secure their spray skirts over the cockpits, and finally, off they go into the current.

In other words, the group river trip process involves many moving parts and could never go unnoticed by local rangers.

On the other hand, Catherine and I were just two kayakers on a self-support trip. Everything we took had to fit into the hull spaces in front of our feet and behind our butts. No sleeping mats, no tables or stoves. No camp chairs. No elaborate meals or cachets of beer. In addition, considering the relative simplicity of our trip, Catherine determined that we could bypass the busy Pump House dock and instead enter the river at the modest Big Gypsum put-in.

We packed up our boats, geared up, and nosed into the river without catching the attention of rangers, sheriffs, or federal search parties. We weren't trying to be sneaky or stealthy. We just were. And I had actually forgotten about the possible river shutdown. So it turned out that while rangers were overseeing the shutting down and dismantling of all those larger river trips they had decided to keep off the river, we inadvertently slipped under their radar.

This stretch of the Dolores River runs alongside the road and then almost immediately veers into a deep, red-walled canyon. Catherine gazed dreamily at the walls. She had the sort of wide smile that could knock anyone into a good mood. And when she was relaxed, which she was on the river, her entire composure would follow suit.

Every time she turned back to look at me, I pretended to also gaze dreamily at the canyon walls, but most of the time, when she wasn't looking, I was struggling just to keep my kayak upright, paddling violently away from rocks and minor riffles in the water.

But in calmer moments, I watched Catherine's poetic paddling. Her strokes were smooth and perfectly timed, letting the fast current pull us, but not spin us, up to the looming canyon sides and around swirling eddies. Watching the methodical rotations of her wrists lulled me into a feeling, just a feeling, of gracefulness.

We pulled into Catherine's favorite campsite, the Tree Camp, so named for the two struggling cottonwoods that provided a rare spot of shade. After we changed into our sandals, we hiked up through the scrub oak brush to look at petroglyphs on the canyon walls.

Due to our limited cargo space, our dinner menu for both nights was freeze-dried refried beans and tortillas, cooked over a small camp stove. We then lay out under the crisp, star-filled desert sky. Catherine said, "Didn't the river seem unusually quiet today?"

"It did," I replied, just then realizing that the river was quiet probably because they had shut it down for the manhunt. I had a sickening feeling in my gut that I should have warned Catherine of that possible scenario. I still said nothing, hoping I was wrong.

But later that night, we awoke to the roar of a helicopter overhead, scanning the canyon with its spotlight. Sitting upright in our sleeping bags, we watched it disappear around the bend in the river. Turning to me, Catherine exclaimed, "What the hell was that?"

I furrowed my brow and stuck out my lower lip. "Um. Come to think of it, I ran into Mark at the Wild Horse. He said the manhunt for those fugitives might be moving to this part of the canyon and that they might block people from going on the Dolores."

Catherine said, "And you didn't think to tell me?"

I smiled sheepishly. "I figured you would know if they shut down the river."

Catherine always seemed to know everything about the Dolores, or any other river, or anything to do with rivers. But I guess I had always been more in the know when it came to crimes and criminals. I said, "I just thought we had a kind of unspoken agreement not to bring up the manhunt. I didn't want to spoil our trip."

She said, "I thought they'd gotten away and were last seen in Wyoming."

I shrugged. "Mark said they found a body near here. Probably the driver. They think the other guys shot him for stopping for the patrolmen, or maybe because he was too fat to move fast enough on foot in the desert."

"Really?" she said.

"But not to worry. Mark lent me his knife." I took out a big, serrated hunting knife and showed it to Catherine with a proud nod.

"Don't they have machine guns?"

I winced.

Catherine lay back down and sighed. "Well, it seems we'll get our pick of campsites."

I stayed awake, choreographing what heroic acts I'd perform should the desperados descend upon us and attack us for our kayaks and freeze-dried beans. Then I snorted and tried to muffle my laughter.

"What's so funny?" Catherine said.

"Sorry," I whispered. "I thought you were asleep."

She snorted. "Are you kidding me?"

"I was just imagining those overweight, camouflage-clad dudes trying to make a break for it in our little kayaks."

"And in your scenario," she asked, "while we were laughing at their awkwardness, were we alive or dead?"

We were subdued and very quiet the next morning, mostly due to lack of sleep. I expected a scolding from Catherine about the manhunt thing, but we just packed up and got back on the river. As before, I followed

Catherine, watching her solid, sure strokes and, every now and then, a cranked turn of her wrist. Her gaze scanned the high, undulating canyon walls.

A bald eagle atop a tree spread its wings and took to the sky. I pointed. "Look!"

She turned around and shushed me. "We don't want to draw any attention to ourselves."

After a day of relatively tame paddling, we pulled into camp. The site was on a mesa overlooking the river and beside a canyon inlet called Coyote Wash. The wash was a narrow stream surrounded by sand and tall rock walls. She said there was a long-standing tradition among river runners of hiking the secluded Coyote Wash topless and stoned. I pulled down my bathing suit. The warm sun fell softly on my bare chest.

Once we were high, the whole fugitive thing seemed funny. We stripped and lay in the hidden little creek and laughed about our situation, the fugitives' semiautomatic rifles versus my fishing knife. Catherine reminisced about how, when she and her friends were younger, they used to play tag, naked, in Coyote Wash. But that was all done with now. Everyone had grown up.

Back at camp that night, I prepared our refried beans and tortillas. We added cheese and spicy salsa, which made the meal seem almost upscale. As soon as the sun dropped below the canyon wall, we went to bed so that our headlamp wouldn't be spotted by either the fugitives or the search parties.

No helicopters came that night. I said,

"Maybe they caught them."

"Hope so."

The next morning, we put in just after sunrise, to the echoing songs of canyon wrens. When we came upon a minor rapid, I followed Catherine into the fast current rushing along the outside bends in the river. We had to lean away from the scooped-out rock walls to keep from bumping our heads.

The most challenging rapid of the trip was just ahead. It was only a Class III, but Catherine said she would go behind me in the role of "cleanup," which basically meant to rescue my boat and me should I flip.

I tried to turn my trepidation into adrenaline as the roar of the rapid grew louder. Then I saw it. "Just one last big one," I thought, as I dipped the nose of my kayak into the tongue.

I paddled fiercely. The rapid had several large waves and holes, and the current veered hard to the left, then right, and then left again. I struggled to move in a sort of squirrelly and determined way in order to both follow the flow and avoid the boulders the flow wasn't avoiding. I was so relieved to get through it without flipping, my face hurt from grinning.

The canyon opened up and we could now see the road. Closer to civilization, Catherine and I spent the next stretch of flat water just laughing and talking. I wasn't intimidated anymore about the kayaking. We shared granola bars and let our boats drift along.

At some point, our kayaks caught different currents. I was on the fast track, sometimes facing forward but mostly backward. Catherine was practicing maneuvers in the slow water when she abruptly called out to me. I glanced up to see her flailing her paddle.

I looked downriver and realized I was heading into a small rapid. It looked to be only a little more than a riffle. I waved to Catherine that everything was okay, then spun my boat to approach the rapid head-on. I paddled hard through some big waves and let the rest of the rapid take me. Then, *crunch!* My kayak hit a mostly submerged boulder.

I used my paddle to brace against the rock in order to stay balanced and upright. The river rushed upon me, suddenly so forceful and constant that I found it hard to breathe. Beginning to panic, I shook my hips and jabbed the rock with my paddle, trying to get unstuck.

Then I saw her boat bearing down on me. Catherine was in a long boat she only took out for self-support trips, because it was so big and unwieldy, a ship compared to the newer playboats. When the bow of her ship struck my kayak, it knocked me off the rock. Now she was on the boulder. I stared at her, and she yelled, "Turn around and watch where you're going!"

I got through the tail of the rapid in seconds and then eddied out to witness Catherine do a complicated maneuver to extricate her boat from the rock and send her back into the current. She came up beside me, panting, and asked if I was all right.

I laughed. "I'm fine!"

She said, "There's nothing funny about what just happened. You have to respect the power of the river and take it seriously."

Having just experienced the force of it pinning me against that boulder, I knew she was right. During the rest of the afternoon, I chastised myself aloud about the incident, hoping Catherine would say something to make me feel better. But she didn't take the bait.

Eventually, I bumped my boat into Catherine's and said, "I just made one stupid mistake."

She said, "Which was your one stupid mistake?"

"You're still sore about the manhunt?" I asked.

"Kind of," she said. "Actually, that was just a questionable decision. But hitting a rock in a rapid, that will get you killed. You have to always be watching for rocks. If I hadn't been right behind you..." Her chin started to tremble, and she swung her kayak back into the current.

I felt like I was no longer under her wing. I was actually being kicked out of the nest.

The takeout was just around the bend. A very miffed ranger was there to greet us. He didn't quite believe that we hadn't known about the river being shut down for the manhunt, but he gave us a pass because it was no longer closed.

He told us the two remaining fugitives had apparently gotten separated during their escape through the desert. The leader, a Durango native, knew the terrain and managed not only to evade capture, but also to flee the area. The other guy, who had minimal desert experience, had probably walked off a cliff during the night. They found his body in a ravine.

The sheriff said, "That greenhorn just didn't have the sense to watch where he was going."

Catherine folded her arms and looked at me. I had obviously been the greenhorn on our trip.

Still, a part of me felt satisfied, elated, really. We'd made it. Evaded disaster. As we packed up under the bright blue sky, with the afternoon sun baking the desert-bronzed rocks, I realized I was actually okay with being kicked out of the nest.

EL CUERPO

As I sat in my bungalow at the university in Honduras, I couldn't stop wondering what was going through Ramon's mind at the moment he started falling. In that instant, when he had a hold on the cliff's edge, did he feel like he might be okay, only for that relief to burst into terror as his hold gave way? Did he struggle as he plummeted those 200 feet? Was that how he lost one of his boots?

It wasn't just my usual journalist's curiosity. Maybe it was a fear of how I will die. Will I be afraid? Will I struggle, or will I just give in to it?

They said Ramon suffered compound fractures in every bone of his body. But they didn't need to tell us that. We could barely keep all of him on our makeshift stretcher as we carried him out of the rainforest.

The Honduran police asked if we had pushed Ramon.

The two girls, who had actually been beside him when he fell, wept in the police station so they didn't have to answer any questions, as if their tears absolved them of all accountability.

My boyfriend, Patrick, and I had travelled from Durango, Colorado, to Honduras to do a story on the international agricultural school. After a few weeks at the university, we befriended one of the young groundskeepers, Ramon. He insisted on taking us to remote places because, he said, we needed to see the side of Honduras not plagued by poverty and corruption.

Although tall and angular in build, he had a very soft, inviting face. The girls, Vanessa and Sylvie, were exchange students from England. Sporting minimal clothes and lovely British accents, they'd captured Ramon's attention. So he invited them on our last day's hike to La Tigra Cascada.

Vanessa was dark-haired and petite, with large brown eyes. Despite her sweet countenance, she was always in charge. Even six-foot-tall Sylvie followed Vanessa like a puppy.

Ramon doted on Vanessa. That day he had insisted on carrying her pink-and-yellow flowered backpack. I remember this detail because we found the knapsack under his body. Inside was her smashed disposable camera and some bug repellent.

We had driven early that morning to La Tigra Rain Forest. The washed-out road wound up a mountain to an abandoned mine. Once we arrived at the trail, Vanessa took the lead, reminding me of a tugboat in front of the big-boned Sylvie, who plowed through the undergrowth ahead of me, sending up a spray of dew and spiders. The forest was dark, the air thick and perspiring.

We reached La Tigra Cascada by mid-afternoon and had our lunch on a flat-topped boulder at the base of the falls, a 200-foot rock face topped with a tangle of vines and brush. In the rainy season, it would be covered with a plummeting froth, but this was May, and only a delicate film of water dripped over the falls.

After lunch, Vanessa stood, brushing off the back of her khaki shorts. She paced with jerky, quick strides, then began fingering the glistening rock face. Satisfied with a couple of handholds, she tested footholds with a boot and raised herself from the ground.

With slow, focused maneuvers, Vanessa, who evidently had some experience rock climbing, pulled herself up to a small ledge eight feet above the ground. I nudged Patrick and said, "That would be a good shot."

He shrugged. "Her clothes blend in too much."

I tugged at my red T-shirt. "Would this be better?"

"I guess," he said.

Being afraid of heights, I wasn't about to climb the rock face. Instead, I veered left, bushwhacking up through the dirt and vines of the jungle. Beside me, Vanessa continued to climb the slick waterfall face.

Sylvie looked up from an attempted conversation in broken Spanish with Ramon, then jumped to her feet. "Jesus, Vanessa, be careful! I don't want to have to carry you out of here."

"Come on!" Vanessa yelled. "It's easy!"

Sylvie and Ramon began to climb. They crawled up past me. I inched out onto Vanessa's previous perch and pretended to enjoy drinking water from the dripping falls, for the sake of Patrick's photo shoot.

I don't really know what happened next. I just know that when I looked up, Vanessa, Sylvie, and Ramon had climbed above me. Sylvie was fearful for her friend. Ramon seemed captivated by Vanessa's daring, and maybe considered this the level of boldness he'd have to display to garner her attention.

I retreated from the rock face and took my time, working my way through the jungle back down to the base. By the time I made it to our lunch spot, Patrick was so intent on repacking his photography gear that he had become completely unaware of anything beyond his equipment bag.

"Where are they?" I panted.

He looked around. "I don't know. They might have gone on."

"Went on where? You didn't see them climb down?"

Patrick shrugged. "Maybe they came down a different way."

"You don't do that," I said. "You don't split up." I was angry at their recklessness but also humbled by their tireless energy.

The density of the rainforest was overpowering. Off the trail, the growth and moisture were so thick it was hard to breathe, much less hear or see anything outside of arm's reach. When we first noticed their disappearance, they could have been anywhere. So, assuming Ramon and the girls had gone ahead on the trail, we did too, at a fast clip, to catch up. And though we continued to call, they never heard us.

Vanessa said later, "We climbed as high as we could. Sylvie and I wanted to get to the top of the falls and wave at you. You know, surprise you. But we got lost in there. Ramon said he thought he knew a way down. He said he'd done it before. We made it to this cliff and could finally see the sky. We were feeling so good. We climbed over to the ledge, and then Ramon got nervous and said something like, 'I don't think anyone has been here before.'"

After a while, Patrick, in the lead, stopped to peel a cobweb from his face. "Well, hell," he said. "I don't know where they are, but I don't think they're ahead of us." He slid the camera bag off his bare, sweaty shoulder, indented red by the strap, and then hoisted the equipment onto the other shoulder. "Let's go back to where we last saw them." Near the base of the falls, we sat on a log and waited.

Patrick asked, "So how should we act when they get back?"

"Mad," I offered. Then I said, "But it's impossible to get mad at Ramon."

Patrick said, "We could brandish him in English and scold the British girls in Spanish."

"How about a universal half-sneer," I suggested. We tried it out and laughed.

Then a scream startled us; a strange scraping sound, followed by cheering. Or more screaming?

A stone plunked to the base of the falls. We turned to it just as something white and flat seemed to float down, ending in a crunching thud. Neither of us moved. A pause, to barely digest the idea that a horrible accident might have just happened.

I was running before I had decided to run, crashing through branches, stumbling over rocks. I stopped when I saw a bare foot.

Patrick ran past me. "Oh my God," he cried. "It's Ramon!"

Ramon's head was hidden, crushed between two boulders. A clean white leg bone stuck out of his jeans. I was vaguely aware that I was shaking. I started to cry but couldn't; I couldn't breathe.

Patrick felt Ramon's neck for a pulse and said, "He's dead."

Thank God, I thought. I turned and turned, trying to get my mind to stop spinning. By the time I calmed down, Patrick had begun turning around. I tried to stop him, but he shook me off. "No, I'm seeing what we have to make a stretcher. Vines. We need to get him out of here before it gets too dark." He had liked Ramon and started swearing at his body for being stupid.

When I removed my windbreaker to help tie the stretcher together, a Snickers bar fell out. I always took a candy bar with me in case I got lost and needed some sustenance. Its presence in my fingers felt obscenely unhelpful. I looked to the top of the falls and said, "Something's wrong."

"I know," said Patrick. "Where are the girls? Can you hear them?"

I shook my head.

Patrick looked to the top of the falls, glowing in the last rays of sunlight. He closed his eyes and sighed. "Goddamnit! I'll go up." He glanced at me. "You stay with the body. In case the girls make it back."

It was startling to me how quickly Ramon went from being a person, a friend, to being a body. *The* body.

"No!" I protested. "You're going to try to be a damn hero and get yourself killed too." I don't know when I'd made the transformation, but I felt that I had just become a bitch. Patrick was a skilled rock climber, even while carrying photo equipment on his back.

During our standoff, Vanessa stumbled out from the thicket.

She saw Ramon and folded to the ground. "Oh God," she choked.

"Up there," she said between gasps, pointing to the top of the falls. "We got cliffed out up there. Ramon tried to jump to the edge... Oh God, he just slipped." She looked at her hands, which were bleeding. "I panicked. I just started climbing. But Sylvie's in shock. She's stuck."

Patrick and I hid our packs and followed Vanessa through the forest beside the falls, scaling the steepest pitches by crawling and pulling ourselves up by vines and tree roots. The clammy air shimmered with an endless weave of spiderwebs. We gave up trying to shake them off. I felt jittery, but when I looked down at my hands, they were steady, on autopilot.

Vanessa turned in toward the falls to a cliff top. Walking to the edge, she called down to Sylvie. Patrick and I stretched out on our stomachs to peer over.

Some ten feet below, Sylvie stood trembling on a foot-sized ledge, bracing her back against the cliff. She was sandwiched between a rock wall and a larger ledge smoothed and glossed by water.

Vanessa pointed a shaking finger to where the water trickled over the ledge and disappeared. "That's where he went over," she said. "He tried to jump over the water to the dirt. But he slipped and fell on the rock and began sliding, right to the edge, then stopped.

He looked so relieved that we laughed. Then he started to slide again. And he was just gone."

She choked on a sob, then rubbed the emotion from her face.

Patrick said, "We've only got about an hour more light, if that." Then he called to Sylvie, "You have to climb up!"

She craned up her sallow face and simply shook it side to side.

"Okay," Patrick said to Vanessa and me. "We'll have to use these vines. There's a bit of a ledge above Sylvie. I'll rappel down to it and bring her up in stages."

"No!" I barked again.

"Believe me, I don't want to do this." His face looked stricken. "But I know I can, so I have to."

While we were binding the vines, a young boy with a machete appeared, hacking his way onto our open ledge. Other shirtless boys followed him onto the cliff top. They said nothing. Three of the boys went to the edge and looked over, nudging one another and laughing.

Patrick rubbed the back of his neck. "What the hell are they doing here?" Then he said to me, "I'll get them to help me. You go back down and guard the body."

"The body?" I said. There it was again. Wasn't Ramon still Ramon for a little longer? Patrick's impatient expression seemed to tighten to the point of explosion.

"Okay," I said. "I'll go down." Then I grabbed his shoulders. "But you don't get stupid up here." He laughed and turned away. I shook him. "No, look at me. I'm serious." But he wouldn't look at me.

Scrambling down the side of the falls, I kept losing my footing, tumbling until stopped by a tree or a withered clump of roots. I met up with a soldier in khaki knickers, a machine gun strapped across his back. He asked me a lot of questions in Spanish, speaking so quickly I couldn't understand. Finally, he shook his gun in my face and barked, "¡Dónde el cuerpo! ¡Dónde!"

I waved him to follow me and continued scrambling down the hill.

Our packs had been ransacked. Some of the onlookers, who'd hiked miles to see the dead body, had left with Patrick's and my passports and money, which we thought we had hidden. Our violated packs lay next to Ramon, and the few people who had remained circled around the body. They hovered and then stooped to get a closer view.

I knelt beside Ramon and our packs, but was too nervous to try to disperse the crowd. All the while, I kept looking to the top of the falls, expecting to see Patrick falling over it. Two men squatted beside me. The larger one waved a thumb back over his shoulder. "Muerto," he said.

I nodded. "Sí."

They said something else to me in Spanish.

"No comprendo," I said. I broke off part of my candy bar and handed it to them.

"Gracias," they said and sat beside me on the log.

The three of us stared at the small crowd and the body, contorted and disfigured, prostrate to the incessant gaze of the living. Occasionally, one of the men beside me would mutter something about *el cuerpo* and *sangre*. But there wasn't much blood. White skin, white clothes, white bones. The only color was the edge of Vanessa's pink-and-yellow flowered knapsack sticking out from under his back.

Night fell. Eventually, Vanessa and Sylvie stumbled from the blackened thicket into our moonlit opening. Sylvie hurried her friend past the body. Patrick appeared next, with the soldier and the entourage of local boys.

We made a stretcher from vines, branches, and spare pieces of clothing. When we lifted the body, Ramon's skeleton crumbled within his skin. We laid him out on the stretcher and, out of some sense of respect, reassembled Ramon's form as best we could. None of the locals helped us. That should have been our first clue that, the way they saw it, Americans had killed a local man.

Patrick took the lead with our only flashlight, shining it behind for me when we had to stumble over rough terrain. Many more witnesses had come to watch.

Behind the trailside branches, moonlit figures, or sometimes just faces, would form as we passed.

A farmer with a flatbed truck met us at the deserted mine. Already, rumor was spreading that Patrick had pushed Ramon. While the men were putting the traumatized Vanessa and Sylvie into the cab, the rest of us piled onto the truck bed. We pushed back against the rickety wood sides as they slid the stretcher, carrying Ramon, in with us. Somehow, I wound up holding Vanessa's backpack.

The truck rumbled forward. Swinging around the first hairpin turn, the boys lurched and laughed, grabbing the truck side. We reached the village at about midnight. A gathering awaited the arrival of *el cuerpo*. As the drunken crowd swarmed our truck, I wished we had thought to cover Ramon's bare foot. The missing boot made him look silly.

Soldiers ushered us into the police station. We sat on benches. Sylvie and Vanessa huddled together, whimpering. My ankles and wrists itched terribly. Patrick also scratched. "Chiggers," he said.

"Chiggers?"

He said, "It's a rainforest thing. They're like fleas, but they burrow under your skin."

The Police Chief, a short man with stern eyebrows, strode into the station. He had just been out to view the body and looked angry. He summoned Patrick into his office.

The soldiers watched the girls and me with cold stares. Machine guns lazed over their laps. Inside the office, the tone grew tense with argument and interruptions. The volume escalated. Our soldiers paced.

After about an hour, the front door opened, and a clearly important person walked in. He was sleepy-looking but immaculately dressed in a crisp, pressed shirt.

He nodded at me, then went straight to the office. As soon as he was inside, the tumult of angry voices simmered down to gentlemanly conversation, mostly in Spanish. Then the important man, who turned out to be the president of the international agricultural school, reemerged with Patrick in tow.

We tumbled into a van and started back toward the school, 150 miles away. We sped, rumbling down the unpaved road, windows open, faces awash in wind and inexorable images. Flower-covered crosses dotted the roadside, marking automobile accidents of days, months, and years past.

I asked Patrick about the interrogation. He laid his head back against the seat and closed his eyes. "They wanted us to confess to pushing Ramon," he said, then looked over at me. "Luckily the university is very powerful around here."

At the infirmary, they took us all to separate showers, where nurses scrubbed us down with wire brushes to dislodge the chiggers. Then they swabbed us with alcohol.

The more the girls whimpered, the more I hated them for it, partly because I blamed them for leading Ramon up the waterfall. For them to cry now seemed self-indulgent and unhelpful. I offered Vanessa the backpack Ramon had been carrying for her, with her now-crushed camera. She said, "Oh no, I couldn't."

That night, Patrick went out with some of the others from the university. I sat on my bed in the bungalow. A breeze rattled the leaves outside, scattering the moonlight across my sheets. The annual onslaught of giant beetles pummeled the window screens.

I kept rewinding the sight of Ramon falling. I wanted to know what he'd experienced; I wanted to know the moment he started clawing at the wet rock face.

Because Ramon's legs were the most damaged, the doctors assumed he had tried to land on his feet. He was

Ramon, trying to land on his feet, seconds before becoming *el cuerpo.*

I searched the room for familiar objects—the green glow of my travel clock, my suitcase—some respite from the darkness. I imagined Ramon's ghost out in the courtyard. I was suddenly afraid of the dark.

I began kneading my thighbone. The thin flesh covering it had been rubbed to numbness by wire brushes. I was feeling for a semblance of living skeleton. I lay back and looked down at my bare feet. I fingered the contours of my arms, my clavicle bones. I felt like a thing. A body. *El cuerpo.* Except that when I touched my face, it was warm and damp with tears.

A PERFECT ROLL

I have made questionable choices when it comes to men. And yet, I was never very understanding when they broke up with me. In fact, the only time I have ever truly appreciated (after the fact) the favor done unto me in the form of a "dumping" was underwater. Actually, the appreciation started just before flipping my kayak.

I was with my friends Kat, Ginny, and Sue. I had just told them I was glad Patrick, an old boyfriend, had dumped me. During my ramblings, I neglected to realize I'd been drifting toward the shore and an "eddy line," where the current changes direction. In a flash, more of a slurp, I was sucked upside down into the river's shockingly cold underwater tumult.

When I first met Patrick in the Grand Canyon, I was married and living in Washington, D.C. It had been a long time since I'd felt any semblance of independence. "Can you stand to be away from your husband for two weeks?" my stepmom had asked when she called about my assisting her on a documentary in the Grand Canyon.

I said, "Yes," but I wasn't quite sure about traveling on my own.

Not until hiking down from the South Rim of the Canyon did I start to feel strong. It wasn't the kind of strength one achieves in frenzied aerobics classes. It was a new kind of strength, a quiet kind, and I liked how it felt.

By the time I got to the bottom of the canyon, I was primed to meet a guy like Patrick, one of the river guides, a rock-climbing, Barry Lopez–quoting, Glenlivet-sipping, tanned mini-Adonis in flip-flops. His jaw seemed permanently gripped from some kind of controlled passion. Over the next eleven days, his provoking questions and amused, striking blue eyes burrowed into me and somehow breathed in new life. I wanted to press my lips to his until his jaw unclenched.

Underwater, in my kayak, all I could think of was that I had not had time to gulp in a lungful of air before flipping over, and that I would need to do at least a sloppy attempt at a roll just to get a breath.

Kayakers roll all the time, to right their boats after flipping. I had practiced, but it never felt natural.

Tucking forward, I pushed my paddle out to the side of my boat, snapped my hips, and then, muscling the paddle down, craned my head up—novice mistake, but I caught a quick gasp of air and a brief onslaught of above-surface cries of encouragement before the river's force took me under again.

With some air in my lungs, I carefully set up my roll for a second try, tucking forward as if to kiss the front of my boat, setting the paddle to my left, reaching up beside the kayak, knuckles feeling the splashing of the river's surface. I swept the paddle headward, then out, snapped my hips, and rolled up.

I was in the world again; Kat and the others paddled toward me, whooping cries of relief that they hadn't had to rescue me, and then yelling something else. I was faced upstream, languidly enjoying the respite, when I backed into a swirling river hole and was yanked under again.

It seemed like the rapid was hissing, *You have no business being here.* It tried to hold me down. I tried a sloppy roll, just to get air, but my paddle hit a boulder and that threw off the sweep. Another attempt. I got a quick gasp of air and heard Kat yelling. Then I went back under again. No underwater quiet as in the flats, just terrifying chaos.

While we were on the Grand, Patrick had said he couldn't understand why I was so timid. Not about the river, in particular, but about everything, heights, scratching my shins, publishing my writing. About wanting a life that made sense to me, even if it made no sense to anyone else. He said, "Go on and get out from under that rock."

I had thought a lot about that phrase during the times Patrick let me row his wooden dory boat through the flat water, those long, hot stretches between rapids. How had I so willingly let the *me* in me fade away?

After the trip ended, my husband complained about my scrapes and bruises. Patrick often phoned from his home in Flagstaff and told me about his adventures.

He once called me while he was on a job photographing an ice-climbing expedition. I could hear the wind howling outside his tent. It made me wonder what being with Patrick would be like—free, rough, passionate. Then he would mention certain ways of improving my marital sex life. But he did it in a flirtatious way.

This went on for a year, as I struggled with my morals, or whatever they were. After all, my "good life" was still salvageable. Patrick and I hadn't actually succumbed to having an affair.

Still, after one marriage counseling session, my husband, confused and indignant, moved into a separate apartment. I packed up my car and headed west. My eyes were trained on Patrick's Arizona beacon, but I knew I needed a town only near enough for visits. My pride insisted that I wasn't moving to be with him. I was moving to be near the feeling of being in the Grand Canyon. I set down fledgling roots six hours north, in Durango, Colorado.

The first time I saw Patrick after the Grand, I was on my way to Durango. We finally consummated our infatuation. It was a little anticlimactic. But life, in general, had become so exciting. We saw each other many times after that; sometimes for fun, and sometimes to join forces on stories, as a photographer/journalist team. When we traveled by car, I drove and he played the guitar, mostly Robert Earl

Keen songs. We camped. Not by the river, though, because "it's too loud," he said. I couldn't imagine thinking a river was too loud.

Then one morning he phoned me from Flagstaff and dumped me. He said he had a hunch it wasn't going to work.

One of Patrick's fellow river guides, Rebecca, told me she had seen him kissing another woman a week before. Rebecca, a blonde like me, also said that she herself had been married when Patrick wooed her and then dumped her for me. A new conquest. That's how I saw it then.

I was furious, of course. As I settled into my new life in Durango, I called him names: bastard, wife-seducer, boater-whore. I must have cried, all while exploring the nearby mountains and learning how to take my bicycle off pavement and into the desert. I started noticing that, with or without Patrick, I was enjoying life and feeling competent.

We still sometimes spoke on the phone. At one point, I told him that I wanted to learn to kayak. On his next trip through Durango, where the rivers are big and not dammed, Patrick brought me a beat-up yellow kayak. He tossed it out of his pickup onto my gravel driveway. Then he looked directly into my eyes and said, "Get in that boat and get that boat on the river!" He gave me an old motorcycle helmet he had painted gold for a Halloween costume.

Patrick had a perfect roll, meaning when his kayak turned over, he could always roll it back up with a true "combat" roll. He could roll up without warning, in a rapid. He could roll up on both sides. He could roll up without a paddle, and one-handed. All this he learned in a pool before ever entering a river. He was determined never to suffer the indignity of swimming out of his boat, the way novices did when they forgot their rolls in the turbulence of a rapid. He was set on never having to be rescued.

So, a year later, I was kayaking down the Dolores River with Kat, Sue, and Ginny, along with a raft of other companions. We floated and paddled between cliffs hollowed smooth by the water flow. I found myself talking about Patrick, not the weepy way I used to go on about his lost love.

I was wearing his ridiculous gold-painted helmet and looked like something to be shot out of a cannon. It felt right. I was here, going down the Dolores River with friends: the severe sun combined with the cool shade from the tall sienna cliffs, then frigid water.

I told Kat that when I got home, I would call Patrick and officially forgive him. I wanted to thank him for loving and then dumping me. I had that bizarre thought in my mind when the eddy line grabbed my kayak and flipped me over the second time. Now I was under again.

My almost-roll had given me only a gasp of air. I was depleted by the initial effort and my own fear. My helmet bumped over the rocky riverbed as I tried to get myself into a tuck and get my paddle to the surface. Suddenly, my helmet jammed on the branch of a submerged tree, thrusting my strapped chin and neck away from my body, which was still being pulled by the kayak in the current.

I let the paddle go and reached for the spray-skirt strap above my knees that would release me from the kayak. But while my helmet remained hinged on the branch and the river's current pulled the kayak from my trapped head, the spray-skirt strap was out of my fingers' reach. I started to panic.

Struggling with my helmet, I knew I probably had only seconds before reaching the limit, the point at which I'd have no more air. Fortunately, Patrick's helmet was old and the strap worn thin. With a couple of tugs, it gave out and released my head.

But I was still upside down in the rapid. I released the spray skirt and must have blacked out. I have a vague recollection of being pulled out of the water by the shoulders of my life vest, so I must not have been entirely unconscious. The rafters hauled me out, and we sailed through the frothy tail of the rapid.

***

Patrick drowned in his kayak that day. He didn't get a chance to roll, but neither did he have to pull his spray skirt and swim. He didn't have to be rescued.

He was on a particularly challenging Class V rapid in California. His companions had decided to walk around it. Patrick, who had soloed through the Grand Canyon, decided to run it. They said he maneuvered through the waves until an unusually violent eddy pulled him backward under the lip of a boulder.

He was close enough to the river's edge that his friends were able to jump in and pull on his kayak. But the force of the Class V rapid, folding back on itself, pinned him in the hole as the waves pummeled him. They yanked so hard on his helmet that they ripped it off, but he remained trapped. They couldn't get him out from under that rock.

By the time the river level dropped, Rebecca was there to watch Search and Rescue extricate him. She said he looked as beautiful as ever, as if nothing had happened.

A challenger of rapids, he died never knowing what it was like to swim one, all that slamming into rocks and choking on waves. Maybe he was spared. Or maybe, because of that damned perfect roll, he never knew the relief of surviving a good bruising.

I went to the memorial, where I and other ex-girlfriends sat on a hill, next to the new one. Because of my close call on the Dolores, I imagined he didn't suffer. Maybe his struggle melded into a sort of hypoxic blackout.

And I couldn't help but think, as I watched the funeral, that he would have liked the image of a tribe of blonde women sitting in the Arizona desert, mourning his death.

SCANDAL

Her ghostly figure stood at the top of the stairs, long silver hair cascading over her shoulders, her white nightgown glowing in the moonlight. I had just come inside, and the winter air turned my breath pale from the front door I still held open.

My black, three-legged dog ascended the steps toward her, as if nothing had happened. I shut the door. My bare feet began to tingle and ache from the thawing.

Daisy said, "What on earth were you doing?"

I had come to Ouray to interview Daisy about her late father and husband. They had both been gold miners in the boom years. The drive from Durango over the mountain passes, even in good weather, was a bit sketchy. Today, it had already begun to snow before I set off, and it was coming down hard when I crested the first pass. Traffic was held up on the second pass because a tourist's rental car had gone over the edge, and

Search and Rescue had to bring up the wreck and people on stretchers. While I waited, I let Ahab out and threw snowballs at him, which he caught in his mouth. Downy snow coated his fur.

When I finally got to Daisy's house, a small, powder-blue building, I left Ahab in the car. This was an interview. Serious business. Ahab was not serious.

I wiped my shoes on the mat, and as Daisy opened the door I brushed off the snow that had already accumulated on my shoulders and briefcase. Judging from the pictures on her front hall walls, Daisy was once very statuesque; a tall Welsh woman with long blond hair. Now, at eighty years old, Daisy had folded in on herself, at least physically.

I interviewed her for two hours, asking about what it was like to be the daughter of a miner, then the wife of a miner, and finally the mother of a miner. Her small blue eyes lit up at times, like when she talked about how her father would snowshoe twenty miles over the mountains to bring Christmas gifts to miners and their families who were snowed in. She said, "Some say my father was a hero. He would say you just did what you could."

She joked about rumors that her father had traded her to her husband in exchange for a donkey. Some of the other miners used to tease Daisy that her father had got the better end of the deal. She smiled. "That was a very good, well-broke donkey." She laughed.

"How did you meet?" I asked.

"Well," she said with a smile, "it was a bit of a scandal."

"You see," she said, "there was this boy who worked with my father. One day I went out cross-country skiing to the creek. I turned around there to go home and, wham! An avalanche came down just in front of me. I was trapped because of the creek and because the debris was too difficult to ski across. I thought that was it for me. But apparently, when I didn't come home, my mother sent that boy to look for me. When I saw him coming up over the slide on his snowshoes, why, that's the sort of thing that can win a girl's heart. He had the most beautiful blue eyes."

"That's a lovely story."

"Yes, but I was breaking all the rules for a young lady by being out there at all, much less without a chaperone. That's why my mother sent the one boy. The truth is, my husband gave Dad his donkey just so we could go on our honeymoon without worrying about who would care for the animal. But all everyone knew was that Dad got a donkey and my husband got me. And that's the story that stuck."

When the interview was over, I realized how thickly the snow was falling. Daisy made a few calls and then informed me that the passes were closed.

She said, "I'll set up a room for you. And then we'll have a nice cup of tea."

"I can get a room in a hotel," I said. I was a professional, after all.

"There aren't any hotels open. Peppermint or chamomile?" She went to a cabinet and brought out a carton of Oreos. Putting them on a plate, she said, "Most kids I know love these."

When Daisy showed me to the guest room upstairs, I asked if my dog could come inside.

"Of course!"

Ahab had trouble with the wood flooring, his three paws sliding every which way. But he managed to scramble his way up to our room.

Daisy loaned me a white cotton nightgown. In it, with my hair down, I felt ethereal; how I once envisioned the image of a good woman. On the guest room dresser was a silver, soft-bristled brush and a silver hand mirror. I used them to brush my hair one hundred times, as I'd seen in old-fashioned movies.

Late that night, a strange sort of siren stirred me awake. The licking brought me to full consciousness. It was Ahab whining to go out for a pee.

I took him downstairs and let him out the front door. He had always stuck close to me, so I was surprised when he took off.

His black fur against the white snow, he disappeared at a dead run down the street. He had to be after a deer or a skunk; either way, this was a disaster and could only get worse if I didn't act fast. I ran after him in my bare feet. Ahab thought it was a game and kept running up and down the snowy side streets. I kept insisting in a husky half whisper, "Come!"

After a few blocks, Ahab finally tired of the game and trotted back to me. I led him back to the house.

When I opened the door, there was Daisy at the top of the stairs. "What on earth were you doing?" she asked.

Panting, I said, "Ahab wanted out and then got away from me. I had to catch him."

"In your nightdress?"

I looked down at the nightgown I was wearing, then up at her in her identical gown, with similarly long, light-colored hair. I glanced behind me into the snow-swept street.

I no longer felt pure, even with my hair having been caressed one hundred times by her silver brush. As she glided back to her bedroom, I stammered, "I don't think anybody saw me."

Daisy turned and sighed. "That's a shame. Could've given folks a new scandal to talk about."

IN THE WIRING

My sister had come to visit before, to check out my new home in Durango. But this time, it didn't matter where I was. This time, my little sister was simply coming to me.

I expect Sarah thought I would make her feel safe, like when she was a little girl. But by the time she came to me, she was beyond the comfort of commiserating and laughing over how messed up our childhood was.

During the three-hour drive from the Albuquerque airport to the Colorado state line, the expanse of sunset-orange buttes, the limitless, raw terrain that opens many confined hearts (as it had mine), overwhelmed Sarah. She hung her hospital-frail arms over her head and mumbled, "I shouldn't have come." When night fell, she unfolded her arms and stared out at the desert blackness. She said, "Will we be there soon? I need to be inside."

As I veered off on what I thought was a shortcut, she said, "Getting lost would be very bad for my mental state." Of course, I proceeded to get lost—only briefly, but as soon as I made that U-turn on a deserted road, she began to cry. Then she folded her arms back over her head.

We finally arrived at my duplex hours later. My big, three-legged mutt, Ahab, bounded up to Sarah, and my sister screamed.

Sarah should have remembered Ahab from her first visit two years before. She had played ball with him, using elaborate windups, reaching her arm high overhead, then twirling it around twice before releasing the ball. Sarah was funny then, sassy and impertinent.

Two years ago, Sarah would have punched me for getting lost, laughed, and then grabbed the map and gotten us even more lost. She was defiant then. And she was oddly elated by the redirection (some would say misdirection) of my life, getting divorced, quitting my "important" job, and moving to a small town my father had never heard of.

Sarah, six years younger than I, was petite, unlike me. She was olive-skinned, unlike me. In fact, she was unlike me. Still, we made a good team. Sarah had few friends of her own, but mine always adored her. They felt as protective of her as I did.

She had always been peculiar—dyslexic, cross-eyed, and she matched her physical difficulties with an endearing aversion to acting normal. I took care of her in the here and now, making her lunches, defending her at school, and reading her bedtime stories, while she took care of my soul, making sure I could always poke fun at myself.

When Sarah came to Durango that first time, she cooked dinner for some of my friends and me. It was a truly disgusting meatloaf. But her whirling-around-the-kitchen culinary etiquette made the entire meal adoringly perfect. That was essentially the last time I saw her in what I considered her true form.

After that first visit, her mood began to darken and deteriorate inexplicably. It took that extra step from quirky to unreachable. Psychiatrists couldn't "put a finger on" why or how it happened. They suggested that maybe it was in her wiring, due to an element of mental illness that hopped through our bloodline. And maybe it just kicked in when she turned thirty, which was how old my mother was when she "lost it."

Sarah's psychotherapy sessions increased to three times a week. They prescribed drugs for depression and anxiety. Words started to confuse her. Instructions became incomprehensible. Sarah was never very good at keeping order, but she lost her job as a teacher's assistant because the challenge of filing sent her reeling to the restroom in tears of anger.

On the phone one night, Sarah told me that a voice inside her, her own voice, kept begging her for peace. She said, "I don't understand why I can't just go." I realized she was talking about suicide. Her desire to "go" seemed to make so much sense to her.

She made me promise I wouldn't tell anyone about our conversation. I don't know if immediately calling our father and stepmother was a betrayal or what she expected of me. They found Sarah, unconscious in her kitchen, slumped against the refrigerator, her wrists slit, and the jagged lid of an opened soup can beside her.

Sarah was bandaged and sent to a mental hospital. She was indignant about not being allowed to go to the bathroom in private. It was as if she couldn't understand the significance of having tried to kill herself.

Eventually, Sarah graduated to a halfway house. That was where she was when she told me her shrink would be going away for a two-week vacation in June.

His impending absence terrified her, so she wanted to come to me.

"Yes, that would be good," I said. I wanted to take care of her and make her better with home cooking, sisterly love, and yoga. She wouldn't feel alone anymore. I could be the switch that made her feel safe and loved.

But when I met my sister at the airport, I began to realize I was way out of my league. The once-strong Sarah dragged a small flight bag behind her, a chenille cardigan hanging off her bony frame. Her swollen eyelids were embedded in a puffy face. I grabbed her collapsible shoulders in a hug. The goop on her short, spiked black hair stained my shirt.

When we got to my house in Durango, I thought for sure the sight of my dog would cheer her up, but Sarah just screamed and turned away.

"Don't you remember Ahab?" I asked. She shook her head.

In the morning, I heard Sarah in the shower, gasping sobs behind the locked door. When she came into the kitchen, she didn't appear as if she'd been crying. Maybe it was like an alcoholic who recovers easily from a drunk; crying had become part of her daily life.

She stared at the sliced avocado I was assembling next to some scrambled eggs. "I can't eat that," she said, closing and flexing her swollen hands. "It's this new drug I'm on." Then she rattled off an improbable, complicated list of foods, including avocado, that could kill her.

I said, "Why wouldn't they send you with a list to give me?"

She shrugged.

I scraped the avocado onto my plate and handed her the eggs. As we ate, I said that maybe we could go for a hike later.

"I'm not very strong," she said, pressing her trembling fingertips into the swollen areas under her eyes, a gesture I soon came to recognize as a signal she was about to cry. As she wept, I wrapped my arms around her. I walked Sarah to her room, and we lay together on the inflated guest mattress until she stopped crying.

Determined to push fresh air into Sarah, I eventually talked her into hiking. It was only when we were outside in the bright sunlight that I noticed how much makeup she was wearing; eyelashes stuck in mascara clumps, black bits dangling off the tips; beige cover-up caked into the creases of her nostrils. I remember wanting to put my hand to her face, maybe even smooth the edges of her rouge.

For the walk, Sarah wore black loafers. She scuffled lethargically up the trail about 100 feet and then stopped to rest. The trees were thick, their shade cool and smelling of drying sap. I asked, "Are you all right?"

"I told you I'm not very strong." Again, she pressed her shaking fingertips into her forehead.

"I'm sorry," I said. "I guess I shouldn't have brought you up here."

Sarah smirked. "Just trying to toughen me up?"

"Oh please." I sat down on a rock.

"You know, I told my therapist how you used to say to me that I needed to learn not to cry, like when Mom was mean to me. My therapist said that was probably the worst advice anyone could have given a child."

"Sarah..."

"What?"

"I was a child, too. I was eleven."

"I was five."

Sarah continued walking and I followed. Mountain bike ruts had hardened into the spring mud. When we got to the creek overflowing with snowmelt, Ahab flopped into it, lapping up the water that rushed past him. Beyond the trees, he and the bridge and the river were cast in the exposed sunlight. On the other side, the trail zigzagged up the shaded side of a ridge.

I jutted my chin upward and said, "This is where I go to cheer me up. There's something about getting up high." I crossed the bridge. Sarah got up and stepped into the sunlight, squinted, then retreated back into the shade. She collapsed on a rock. A dripping Ahab ran up to her and dropped at her feet with a groan. I went back for Sarah, yet when I put my hand on her back, it heaved as she started to cry. We turned around and went home.

The next morning, I awoke to the touch of Sarah's fingertips passing over my cheek. Her trembling strokes felt more like a kind of kneading. She said, "I think it's best if I go back. I almost tried to kill myself last night. And I don't want to do that to you."

I didn't try to talk her out of leaving. I'd given up on the absurd idea that fresh air and home cooking could help her. In fact, I felt so ineffectual that I was relieved she had somewhere else to go.

Sarah was quiet most of the drive back into New Mexico. I concentrated on the roadsides, looking for deer that might bolt in front of our car. Coming upon a rumbling, smoking Bonneville, I flicked on my left blinker to pass it.

Sarah said, "I don't blame you."

"For what?" I asked, pulling into the oncoming lane. The Bonneville sped up, trying to incite some sort of race. With traffic approaching, I pressed the gas pedal and sped up around the smoking car.

She said, "I shouldn't have expected you to know how to take care of me."

"Well, I screwed up, I guess. You know, the older I get, the more I realize how young I was back then."

Sarah was looking at me so hard I couldn't help but turn to meet her gaze. She said, "I meant this week. The food, the hiking. I should have made it clearer that I'm really not well."

"Oh," I said. Then I looked back at the road and swerved around a scrap of blown-out tire. We drove past a teepee rest stop. Cantinas and rundown gas stations dotted the sides of the highway. I said, "I'm sorry."

About a mile ahead of us, an old green Nova pulled over and something was held out of the passenger window and then dropped. As we approached, I realized the "thing" was a puppy. I veered off onto the shoulder and got out.

The puppy trotted onto the highway. It crossed between swerving cars to the median. When I got to the median, the puppy had already made it to the other side of the highway.

I ran across and jogged into the scrub oak and cactus, following its whining. Its cries made the desert seem haunted. The puppy wouldn't stop moving away from me, pleading in its cries for help but too afraid to actually surrender. Maybe it was afraid I'd tell him he needed to learn not to cry.

I finally realized I had to give up the chase or make Sarah miss her plane. When I got back to my car, Sarah said, "We're not going to get there in time."

"Yes, we will," I said, peeling out in dramatic, pebble-flinging fashion. I wove through the traffic. "I'm sorry," I said. "I had to try." Sarah snorted a laugh and then wiped her forearm across her nose. With snot smeared across her thick makeup, she said, "Forever the patron saint of lost causes."

Two weeks later, my father called in the middle of the night to say that Sarah had suffered a massive brain aneurysm. At first, I thought maybe it was an attempted suicide by avocado; it would have been like her to go for the absurd. But there had been no apparent cause. One moment she complained of a headache, then suddenly she couldn't speak.

Later, when I called Sarah at the head-trauma hospital, I could tell she was listening because I could hear her breathing. I said, "Do you remember when we went to the river? The first time you came to visit. The river was high. The biggest rapid was overturning rafts of tourists. You thought that was hysterical."

Over the phone, I heard a chortled, fast breathing, a kind of laughter.

I remembered that day so well, beside the river, during her first visit. Sarah had been wearing a floral baby-doll dress. Sun glinted around her silhouette.

She kept running with Ahab to catch the tennis ball before it rolled down the riverbank. He'd always get it first, but she'd dupe him into giving it to her, and they'd run back toward my friends and me sitting on a nearby bench.

Ahab careened into her spindly legs as he jumped for the ball she teasingly kept just out of his reach. Then came another of her elaborate windups, Ahab hopping and falling over in anticipation. The more Kat, Sue, and I laughed, the more Sarah hammed it up.

After Sarah threw the ball and Ahab caught it for about the thirtieth time, Ahab was finally out of breath. He trotted down to the river and plopped into a foamy eddy of backward-swirling water. Sarah jump-jogged down the bank and plopped into the eddy beside him.

I'll never forget Ahab's expression—eyes wide, brows lifted—as he looked at her and then at me, as if to ask, "Is she going to be all right?"

THE GRAVEYARD SHIFT

Walking down the sidewalk next to Ginny and Sue, I felt very tall compared to my tiny, badass friends. I was reminded of the pictures from my trip to the Amazon after separating from my husband. I thought I had mixed well with the Peruvian family who took me into their home, but in the Christmas Eve pictures of us dancing—siblings and parents and grandparents and grandchildren—there I am, sticking up in the middle, a big, gyrating, pale monolith.

Coal smoke encompassed the Colorado horizon beyond Main Street as Durango's narrow-gauge tourist train docked for the night. In the mountains beyond town, burgeoning storm clouds prepared to let loose an evening torrent, first turning delicious shades of red and orange.

Ginny and I had just helped Sue move out of the home she had shared with her husband. Sue's new apartment seemed so barren. I wondered what her first night alone would be like. Maybe Sue would take my advice and sink into a warm bath with a glass of wine and some Kalamata olives, like I was told to do by a fellow divorcée when my husband and I split. Or, in between those lusciously quiet evenings, would she clasp her face in her hands and cry, looking up when she was finally empty, to discover that the sun had set and she was sitting alone in an apartment devoid of any signs that she was ever connected to someone?

Ginny pinned down her skirt as a cold breeze struck us, whipping her long, dirty-blonde hair around her face. We were on our way to a restaurant where a bartender, whom Ginny liked, might be working his usual shift.

Sue said, "I think I'm going to buy a whole bunch of candles."

"Have you gotten a divorce lawyer yet?" Ginny asked.

Sue bunched her hands into fists and pressed them against her chest. "Don't start with that now," she warned, her deflated hands falling by her sides.

Ginny shook her head. "Sorry. Subject dropped."

We walked in silence, and I felt the need to create a distraction. I said, "Did I ever tell you about how I met Ryan McCarthy?"

Ginny shrugged. "I don't think so." We crossed Sixth Avenue, behind a passing pickup truck.

"I was pretending to be someone else," I said.

Ginny laughed. She had this odd ability to squint while keeping her eyes wide open. She turned to walk backward. "Is that how you usually pick up men?"

Sue poked my side a little too hard. "Do tell!"

I felt like saying, *Don't EVER poke me.* But I calmed that city side of me. I felt like a pound dog between two Chihuahuas. "My roommate and I decided to go to her brother's graduation party at a university in a different state, two hours away. On the drive there, we came up with this insane idea that we should make up characters for ourselves. We wouldn't know anybody at the party except her brother, so we could pretend to be entirely different people. I decided to be Zan."

"Zan?" Ginny asked while we waited to cross Fifth Avenue.

"I was a total sexpot."

They laughed.

"What's so funny?" I barked. "I can be sexy!" Ginny and Sue nodded at me disingenuously. I said, "I thought it would be funny to be really bold and racy and flirty, just for a night."

Sue wagged her eyebrows toward Ginny. "And you pulled it off?"

"We got to the party, and I was wearing this black, fuzzy, touch-me sweater. The whole way we made our entrance was different from how we would have normally walked into any other party. We did this hip-swaying, chin-up, challenging, groping-eyes, dead-on kind of walk."

Sue accelerated ahead of us with an exaggerated wiggle. She jumped and turned to face us. "Like that?" she laughed. Sue was a finely tuned athletic machine, with curly, bobbed brown hair. She was very pretty, but not sexy.

"Anyway," I said, "I went from guy to guy, joking and drinking and sticking my boobs out. My roommate and I egged each other on."

At Fourth Avenue, Ginny grabbed Sue's arm to keep her from walking in front of a car. We paused for a break in traffic, then crossed. To the north, in the La Plata Mountains, a scraggly lightning bolt skittered across the darkening sky. Erupting thunder rattled us, and we moved our shaken bones across the street.

"So," I said, "there were these two guys at the party who were after me, or rather, my persona. I flirted between them, and toward the end of the evening—it was a sleepover kind of thing—I decided to fool around with Ryan, the shy one. He was kind of intense, but floppy."

Ginny furrowed her brow. "Floppy?"

"Yeah. He had dark, curly black hair that was all over the place. But he also had these piercing blue eyes. If I saw those eyes today, I'd say they were cold, or mean, but at the time they looked deep. Back in those days, I was attracted to what I took to be symptoms of an untapped depth of character."

Ginny lifted her face to the sunset glow and groaned. "Oh no! Not the cold, silent type!"

"Exactly." I'd always thought that if a guy was reserved, he was preserving the sanctity of some huge bounty of knowledge and underpinning pain. I didn't realize that some guys don't speak much because they have little to say, or, in Ryan's case, because he didn't think highly enough of the human race to engage it in conversation. Anyway, Ryan was, that night, a tempting mystery lying on a little bunk bed in one of the back rooms. "I went and lay down with him."

Ginny laughed. "You slut!"

"Nothing much happened." I waved my arm, encouraging them to keep walking. "In the morning, my roommate and I were up and out of there before the others awoke."

"That's cold," Sue said.

"I know. But I was kind of thinking I'd never see him again. And that wasn't hard to do. I mean, he didn't even know my real name."

"Then a couple of years later..."

"Ah, the plot thickens," Ginny sighed.

"I was working for a magazine in New York, and I ran into Ryan at a hot dog stand. I barely recognized him because he had become an investment banker; he had crew-cut hair, a suit and tie, and a broad-shouldered cashmere coat. He looked scary handsome. As soon as I remembered how I knew him, I wanted to run away, but he gave me a big smile and said, 'Zan?'"

"No!" Sue yelped.

"I eventually explained the whole story to him, and he mostly stopped calling me Zan, but I don't think he ever believed it. Can you blame him? I mean, who assumes alternate personas just for a brother's graduation party?"

Thunder growled low and steady through the valley, followed by a boom that knocked us into each other.

Sue screamed and adhered herself to my side. I put my arm around her, but she shrank away while letting go of me. I wanted to quickly mask the awkward moment. "So, anyway," I said, "Ryan asked me out."

Across Main Street, the moon shivered a vibrant halo within blackening clouds. "Those days, I worked the graveyard shift at *Time* magazine."

Sue stopped, and we paused around her. She furrowed her brow, looking up at me. "You wrote obituaries? How sad."

"What?" I asked.

The wind scattered Sue's bangs across her eyes. "The graveyard," she said.

"No, the graveyard shift. That just means I worked nights and the odd hours nobody else wanted to work. In fact, I worked during the biggest hurricane to ever hit New York City."

Sue rubbed her eyes. "And you're going to tell us all about it."

"The magazine still had to go to press, so we were told that all 'essential' employees had to stay, while the rest should evacuate. My boss dubbed me essential and skipped town.

"I was on the thirty-eighth floor. The wind blew so hard, the building swayed and creaked." I remembered standing in my boss's office, kind of reveling in being deemed essential, and watching garbage and garbage cans flying by. Across several avenues, atop a building being demolished, a wrecking ball swung wildly. When my boss's windows started rattling, I went back to my little cubicle.

"Ryan called, and when I answered, he said, 'So I guess that wasn't you I saw flying past my apartment.' We actually went out for about two years."

Ginny turned her attention to Third Avenue's busy traffic. Noting a break, she hurried us across to the median. After a few more cars passed, we carried on.

"I don't get it," Sue said, stepping onto the sidewalk and looking up at me. "You lied to him."

"Yes, but only at first." I envied her deep belief in her own moral compass, or maybe her disdain for the mismanagement of others' moral compasses.

She said, "How can you build a relationship based on a lie?"

I stopped and spread my arms out. "Do I look like I'm in a relationship?" The only reason Ryan and I lasted so long was because I worked nights and Ryan worked a normal schedule. We basically only saw each other on Sundays, in front of his TV.

A lot of baseball, beer, sex, and pretzels, usually in that order. Then it was football, then basketball. We never had to make or cancel plans to go out. So maybe the key to a lasting relationship is lying and for one person to work the graveyard shift."

"He didn't mind your schedule?" Sue asked.

"No. My whole point is that he liked it. But my job got kind of crazy sometimes."

Ginny rolled her eyes. "Wow. Do tell!"

Sue snorted.

"Seriously, it did!" I felt that surge of adrenaline I used to get every weekend as we tried to get the next issue to press on time. And with the adrenaline came a layer of self-importance I had to shed when I left my job. "One night, actually, it was about 2:00 a.m., I know it was a Sunday morning because we had just 'put the magazine to bed.' Then a message came over the wire. There had been an incident in Beirut, a bombing, maybe a couple of people dead. Then the faxes started rattling in.

"It was the Beirut bombing. We called all the editors and stopped the presses. Everyone at the magazine, including peons like me, worked around the clock to get the story on the cover."

Sue shrugged. "I don't see why it would be such a big deal what was on the cover."

I said, "It was *Time* magazine. And this was probably the worst terrorist attack ever on a U.S. embassy. It mattered!" I breathed in the cool Durango air, breathed it in deeply, trying to remember that that was an entire lifetime ago and in a different universe.

We walked in silence. I had gotten us off the subject of Sue's divorce, but maybe it was time to wrap it up, judging by the waning interest in my Ryan McCarthy story. "But there's more," I said. "By the time I finally got home, I had crossed over into a state of quasi-delirium. I put a frozen pizza in the oven, not noticing the pilot light had gone out, and I lay down."

"With the pilot light off, the oven emitted carbon monoxide into my tiny, gross, one-room apartment."

"Why was it gross?" Sue asked.

"You know she's going to tell us," Ginny laughed.

I did feel the need to explain. "It had a big hole in the floor that bugs used to crawl out of; huge, tank-like bugs. The shower was right next to the kitchen sink. My bed was right next to the gas-leaking stove. So, I went into a very deep, deep sleep."

"Oh no!" Sue exclaimed, stopping and touching her mouth.

"No, this is good," Ginny said. "The heroine of this story must be tired... by now." She laughed.

"Eight hours later," I said, "when I didn't show up for work and they couldn't reach me, they called Ryan. He went over to my apartment and finally broke in.

There I was, a drooling Sleeping Beauty in need of a bath and fresh clothes. I had a splitting headache for days after that. And I got a reputation at work for the most unusual late excuse." I sighed. "It's amazing I ever got promoted to day shift, but that promotion was also the beginning of the end for Ryan and me."

"The end?" Ginny and Sue smiled at each other.

"Sort of. I started to cook him dinners."

"Oh no!" Sue groaned.

"He was the first man I ever cooked a meal for. I went out and bought a steak. I got it in my head that I would cook it in a red liquid to make it juicy. So, I boiled this slab of meat in tomato sauce for about an hour."

Sue covered her face. Opening her hands, she said, "Was it terrible?"

Ginny rolled her eyes. "Duh."

"It was curled up like old shoe leather. Really awful. But Ryan ate it, and he pretended to like it. I mean, how could you not love a guy like that?"

Ginny and Sue shrugged and nodded.

"I didn't mean to sabotage our relationship. I just got put on a normal schedule and suddenly, I was around. Me. My presence in the evenings, not just on Sundays. On Friday nights, I'd get dressed up and go to meet Ryan at his place, and then he wouldn't want to go out. He wanted to just stay in and watch baseball. I was coming off two years on the graveyard shift. I needed air. And a little romance would have been nice too."

Ginny grabbed Sue's arm to steer her around a signpost.

"I remember going downtown to Ryan's apartment after I'd worked all day and noticing for the first time how bad it smelled. Like mold, and takeout Chinese food, and stale beer.

It got up to 110 degrees that summer, and he didn't have an air conditioner. The lights were off to minimize the heat. I joined him on the couch in front of the glowing TV. At one point, I got up to go into the kitchen. When I turned on the light, cockroaches scattered. I mean, that's what really went wrong for us, turning on the lights."

A gust of wind swooped in from behind as we turned onto College Drive. Ginny held down the back of her skirt.

I let my face drink up the moist air, which smelled rich and sweet and foreboding. Sue rubbed her arms, goosebumps bristling in the cold wind. Ginny took a skipping step and turned to walk backward. "Can we pick up the pace? It's about to rain."

As if on cue, a brief flush of rain splattered across the sidewalk. I wiped the drops from my forehead and said, "I'm done. The end."

Sue stopped. "Wait. So that's it? What happened to Ryan? Why is he important?"

I cocked my head. "I don't know. And I think they're all important. Even the ones that don't work out."

Sue nodded. "I guess so."

Ginny looked up into the raindrops. "Jeez, you could have just said that."

The clouds suddenly opened and let loose a torrent. We kept walking at our same pace, despite the soaking downpour. It was monsoon season, after all. The rain was inevitable. What was the point of trying to stay dry?

STEP AWAY FROM THE PUMPKIN

My boyfriend, Larry, unloaded the dishwasher very loudly, slamming coffee mugs on the countertop and dropping the cutlery into a clanking pile above the drawer. I knew he was making all that noise on purpose because he had great disdain for the TV show I was watching, *Law & Order*, which he deemed gratuitously gory.

Larry didn't understand how I could spend my days in the Colorado sunshine, kayaking and hiking, then spend evenings indoors in my dark living room watching a crime drama set in my former home of New York City. Hadn't I moved to Durango to get away from all that?

It's true that *Law & Order* is a gory and violent show, featuring all sorts of despicable behavior. But it spoke to me, somehow, to a familiar mindset I never completely discarded when I left the city.

***

I had moved to New York after college. The only apartment I could afford was a five-story walk-up in what was known as the German ghetto. The floor was so warped that when I laid a pen on my table, it would roll off onto the floor, then across the thickly painted boards until it finally bumped into my shower beside the kitchen sink. It was an illegal sublet I rented from a Turkish man who, I later learned, was a drug dealer called "the Turk."

One night, after leaving my night job at *Time* magazine, I got to my building around 6:00 a.m. Walking up the stairs, I came across a body leaning against the wall, legs splayed. I stepped over him and ran up to my apartment to call 911. Then I walked back down and sat, looking into his unblinking eyes, until the ambulance came to get him.

For my daily sustenance, Triscuits and Amstel Light, I shopped at a small market on the corner until I found its front blocked by yellow police tape.

It turned out the market had been just a front for the Turk's drug operation. I was probably one of only a few customers who actually bought food there. I'd often wondered why the shelves of groceries were always covered with dust.

***

In the kitchen, Larry wrestled with pot tops in the broiler pan drawer. I turned up the TV volume to catch the crux of Detective Briscoe's interrogation as he slammed his fist on the table and shouted, "Admit it! You knew what was going on all along!"

Outside, it was beginning to snow, softly falling flakes against the cool, dark night.

***

In New York, after working for a year at *Time*, I had upgraded my living arrangements by co-renting a "railroad" apartment, which is essentially a narrow train of rooms that dead-ends. In our case, you'd open the front door into the kitchen, go through my bedroom, then my roommate's, and end up in the living room, which was over our landlord's Italian restaurant. Without air conditioning, Gramicci's smells, sounds, and cockroaches came in through the open window.

One night, the restaurant shut down early, but then filled with a stream of loud Italian men. Mr. Gramicci came up to our apartment to borrow some chairs. All we had were two swivel desk chairs, but he took them anyway.

Late that evening, we went down to collect them. Because the restaurant was closed, we went in through a private side door in the lobby, which led into the restaurant's bar. It was dark, but we could tell there had been some sort of tussle because of the broken bottles and overturned barstools. As we rounded the counter, my foot slipped on something wet, and I looked down at a streaked patch of blood. We stumbled back up to our apartment. (The chairs were brought back to us later.)

***

At the refrigerator, Larry put a large metal martini shaker under the ice dispenser, and the cubes clattered in. On the TV, a teary woman said something heartfelt, but I could only catch snippets as Larry shook his cocktail. I turned up the volume. Detective Benson was hunched over, hands on her hips, shaking her head. "So, you stabbed her because Daddy didn't approve?"

***

My living conditions improved considerably when I moved in with an old college friend. Our place was technically a five-story elevator building. However, it had the sort of elevator that required you to manually slam the grate door closed, then throw your entire weight into opening it. And many times, it stopped between floors, requiring tactical maneuvers to get out. But our apartment was a two-bedroom for only $1,600 a month, which was a bargain back in the '80s.

My friend was a promoter for a jeweler and was sometimes paid under the table in uncut baubles. I was always amused by the lengths she went to in order to hide her gems inside fake fruit, fake mayonnaise jars, and hollowed-out books. I thought she was a little paranoid. Then we came home one night to find the apartment in shambles, not just normal robbery stuff like ransacked drawers. The food in the refrigerator had been hacked to pieces, the mayonnaise jar smashed, and the bookcase overturned. The only bauble they missed was the sapphire my friend had taped to the inside lid of the oregano spice jar.

The robbers' muddy footprints documented their path from linen shelves to lingerie drawers and then out the alley window. The police said they probably climbed in from the roof and then rappelled down to the pavement.

After the police left, we discovered a vial of crack on our living room floor beneath the window. We figured it had fallen from one of the robbers' pockets. Afraid they'd come back for it, we placed the vial on the ledge just outside the alley window. Either they, or the wind, eventually took it.

***

The *Law & Order* episode ends, as usual, with the most guilty-seeming man, the husband, being innocent. It's always the soft-spoken, seemingly innocuous person who turns out to be a pathological, lying, misogynistic, megalomaniacal sadist. The district attorney, Jack McCoy, walks down the hall with his assistant and quips something about how nothing is ever as it seems.

Then, the *Babump!* sound and the switch to *Law & Order: SVU*, accompanied by the deep, ominous introduction, "In the criminal justice system, sexually based offenses are considered especially heinous..."

As the *Law & Order* Halloween marathon continued, my boyfriend groaned and ran the disposal.

On the TV, a frumpy Hispanic woman ascends the front steps of a nice brownstone building. She unlocks the door and enters. After the housekeeper takes off her coat, she calls, "Mrs. Montgomery?" then walks into the living room. It's a mess. She groans, "Ah no, always with the parties!" Then she notices the bloodied and naked dead woman splayed behind the coffee table. Big scream.

Our dishwasher went into full swing. I turned up the TV. Detective Stabler is asking a question; however, in my living room, with the revved-up volume, it felt more like screaming, "What time was that!?"

My dog, Ahab, sat up and perked his ears. I imagined he was responding to the TV voices and not the knock of a trick-or-treater. We lived at the end of a long, deserted road. Our house never got trick-or-treaters. Ahab's jowls contorted into a growl. I thought maybe he sensed deer in the yard. Every evening, around that time, a young buck would jump over the fence to munch on the grass beneath our willow tree. Because of the willow's thick branches, this was the only area of the lawn not dusted with snow.

Detective Benson scoffs, "That's one for the record books!"

***

One of the highlights of working in New York was going to summertime baseball games, played in the relative cool of the evening. Coming back to Manhattan after a Yankees doubleheader one time, I stepped off the subway train onto an empty platform. Suddenly two young guys came running out of the men's room. Behind them, an old man in rags stumbled out with a knife sticking out of his stomach, blood oozing.

I don't know why I didn't do more for him, but I hailed a taxicab and gave the driver $20 to drop him off at an emergency room.

***

I muted the TV when an ad came on. We had a moment of relative peace. Then, abruptly, Ahab started barking as if we were under attack. Larry headed toward the entranceway but hesitated when someone pounded on the door with an aggressive "Thud! Thud! Thud!"

I got up, trying to comprehend who could possibly be pounding on my door. I went to get the machete I'd bought while on assignment in Honduras. I sidled past Larry toward the front door. My heart was racing. Through the peephole I saw a masked figure backing away.

I opened the door, machete poised. As the masked person ran off, I followed him out. He jumped into the passenger seat of a pickup truck, then sped off. On my doorstep was a pumpkin, its hideously carved face broiling with fire inside. Coming up beside me, Larry said, "Oh, a pumpkin," and bent toward it.

I side-armed him back behind me. "Honey, step away from the pumpkin." I asked him to put Ahab back inside the foyer.

With adrenaline pumping through my shaking hands, I braced for an explosion as I used the tip of my machete to pop off the top of the pumpkin. A candle flickered in the breeze. But I still didn't trust the pumpkin or the intentions of the person who had mysteriously brought it to my house. I closed the door and went back to watching my crime drama.

About an hour later, my friend Ginny called. "What happened tonight?" she asked and laughed.

"What do you mean?"

"My nephew brought you a pumpkin. He and his dad deliver carved pumpkins to people every Halloween, and I asked him to put you on their list. He said you came after him with a huge knife." Silence. She continued, "I told him he probably imagined it."

"Well, it was a machete, and I didn't actually go after him," I said. "He had a mask on. And he pounded on the door so loudly I got nervous."

"It was a pumpkin!" she laughed. "It's Halloween! People in masks knock on doors."

"Not mine."

The next year, on Halloween, Ginny called to warn me that her nephew would be dropping off a pumpkin. The surprise was usually the most entertaining element of this annual ritual. But apparently her nephew decided that the surprise factor wasn't worth getting stabbed over.

YOU NEW PEOPLE

Jeff had put in for his permit to run the Grand Canyon long before he'd even met his wife, Lorna. He had already invited all his old college buddies. But Lorna was allowed to choose one friend, and that was me, probably because we were both fairly new to Durango and on the same recreational soccer team. Lorna said I could look forward to a fun trip because Jeff's friends were really "casual."

I couldn't go for the full eighteen days, so I worked out a plan with Jeff to send my provisions ahead to be on the rafts when they shoved off. Then I'd hike in on day eight to meet them at the Pipe Springs trailhead. So, at 4:00 a.m., in late June, I descended into the Canyon with a headlamp to guide my way.

Because of our early morning rendezvous, I chose the quickest and steepest route down. Several times, my feet slid out from under me. The rocky terrain rattled my knees and ankles. The grade began to level as the sun rose, charring the cliffs red.

I reached the river at around 7:30. It was still another two miles upriver to the meeting spot. The canyon temperature was predicted to reach 120 degrees that day, and it was already getting hot. My thighs shook from fatigue, and my right knee ached.

I stopped at the worn desert ground of what I thought was the Pipe Springs trailhead, but there was no sign. I set my orange knapsack against a rock to signal my location to the rafters, and then lay down. After a few hours, with no trees for shade, I used a couple of shirts to rig a tarp between two bushes.

I awoke to flies picnicking on my damp forehead. The afternoon sun had shifted around the tarp, and I was getting burnt. I walked into the slow-moving edge of the river to cool off. *Was I in the right spot on the right day?* I wondered. *Had they forgotten about me?* With only a few sips of water left, I began to worry. The heat was claustrophobic. I rearranged the tarp and crawled under it again.

I must have dozed off, because the next thing I knew, a wet sandal was pressing into my shoulder. A large head said, "So sorry to disturb your nap, but some of us have a rapid to run." I sat up and realized it wasn't the head that was so big, but the woman's heap of gnarly auburn hair.

I said, "Was I in the wrong place?" I could barely stand.

The woman, called Dana, said, "No, you were in the right place. We were in the wrong place. But I'm still pissed off." Then she stomped away and lit a cigarette.

Another rower, Heather, hopped off her raft in order to pee in the river. I was so dazed from dehydration, I must have been staring at her, because she looked up from her squat and said, "Are you all right?"

I shook my head. "No."

She dunked her butt into the river and then stood. Tying up her shorts, she said, "You don't look so good. Come with me." She led me to the shade under her boat's umbrella.

Heather was small, strong, and browned from guiding river trips. She had a patch over one eye from a recent flip in a rapid. As she pulled granola bars and a water bottle from the hatch, she explained that she was having a streak of bad luck on the river.

Jeff's boat pulled up. My friend Lorna hopped out and tied the bowline around a bush. The hug she gave me was almost too clingy.

"You okay?" I asked.

"No big fights yet," she laughed. Almost the physical opposite of her long-legged, lumbering husband, Lorna was short and cherubic, with curly blond hair bunched into a ponytail. She said, "We're doing Crystal this afternoon. We've gotten a late start, so I hope you're ready to roll."

Crystal Rapid is one of the canyon's most challenging rapids. I remembered it well from my first trip down the Grand Canyon. One doesn't usually run a rapid like that in heavy hiking boots, in the case of a flip, you might as well be wearing cement blocks.

I said, "I need to get at my river shoes. They're in my dry bag."

"Your dry bag is on my boat," Dana said as she passed. "And I'm not going to de-rig just for you."

"But I got here hours ago," I said.

"Well, as far as I'm concerned, you're not even supposed to be on this trip. It was Jeff's permit."

I turned to Lorna, expecting her to say something on my behalf, but she just looked away. Then she tried to appease me by saying, "It'll be great. You're going to be on Heather's boat."

"The gal with one eye and the bad luck streak?" I asked.

Lorna crinkled her nose and shrugged. "Yeah. But she's really good."

What I didn't know then was that Lorna putting me, her friend, on Heather's boat, despite Heather's blind eye, was an affront to Dana's boating ability.

Just above Crystal, we got out and scouted the rapid from a higher ledge. It was big and loud. Back in the river, we plunged into the tongue of the monstrous rapid. I grabbed the front ropes to "high side" my weight against the oncoming waves. I looked back at one-eyed Heather. She smiled broadly as she rowed through the tumultuous water and churning eddies without a hitch. She yelled over the roar, "Lorna said you'd have a good influence on me!"

"How's that?" I yelled.

Just past the bottom of the rapid, she let her raft spin into an eddy.

"You're calm."

"Heat stroke can have that effect."

She laughed, and we looked back up the river to watch Buck and Jilly, two other rowers, run Crystal. Buck was a massive, red-cheeked man who wore a tattered straw cowboy hat. He muscled through a bad run, with Jilly on the bow, high-siding and screaming into each wave as it smashed against her face. Next were Jeff and Lorna, then Jo-Bob and Connie, who did a lot of whooping and howling.

Buck and Jilly eddied in beside us in time to watch what little we could stomach of Dana's run. Barely rowing, Dana bumped into a rock, which spun her raft around. Continuing to not row, she finished Crystal backwards, looking frantically over her shoulder.

Buck shook his head, saying, "I think she just gets too scared to move a muscle."

At camp, Dana sat on my dry bag on her raft. She smoked her Marlboros and drained another can of Coors while I waited for her to move off the boat so I could get at my bag and finally change out of my boots, the boots I'd been hiking in for hours that morning, baking in for hours, then getting drenched in Crystal.

I said, "My feet are killing me. I need to get inside my dry bag."

She said, "I have my routine. I know Lorna invited you, but you can't just show up and expect me to change my routine."

An hour later, the sun was setting, and the canyon glowed orange. A wren warbled over the roar of the river. My knee had begun to swell. What had been a simple twist was, without Advil, becoming a painful injury. And still, Dana's butt blocked the way to my dry bag. I was tempted to knock her into the water. But being the new person on the trip, I figured it was up to me to make the situation work.

She eventually got off her ass. The cooking area started coming to life, a large tarp was spread on the beach, held in place with rocks, along with a couple of two-burner propane stoves on legs. I had heard someone say earlier that this would be "100% naked night." I'd hoped they were joking, but three of the four assigned cooks for that night began to disrobe. The fourth was Dana. She took off her clothes and yelled, "Swampers!"

Lorna and Jeff had organized the trip so that different cooking and swamping crews alternated daily. Cooks cooked, and swampers did everything else, including setting up the groover, which is like an outdoor port-a-potty.

Lorna was the head of our crew, and we were supposed to swamp that night. But I'd just seen Lorna run up the side of the barren cliff in tears, with Jeff in quick pursuit. Heather, also in my crew, was tending to her eye while there was still light. Connie had set up the groover near the rocks at the river's edge, then went off with Jo-Bob to argue about something.

I went over to Buck, whose eyes were glazed from dipping into his second six-pack of the day. I said, "They keep calling for the swampers, and I don't know what that means, so I just stand here while they yell at me."

He smiled. "Where's the rest of your crew?"

"A couple of them are off crying. And I'm about to join them."

Buck shook his head, his cheeks glowing in the firelight. "Nah, take it easy. We're not all bad. Come on, I'll show you the ropes."

So, I made it through the night. And I still held onto the hope that this trip might become wonderful, like my first time. It was the Grand Canyon, after all.

The next morning, Dana made an announcement at breakfast and prefaced it by saying, "This is directed especially at you new people." Then: "If you make a mess on the groover seat, you have to clean it up."

I turned to Lorna. "I'm the only new person, and I haven't even used the groover yet."

"Oh," Lorna laughed. "Don't worry. Everyone knows who it was. He's been doing it the whole trip."

Later, on the raft with Heather, I asked, "What the hell is the matter with Dana? Why would she say, 'Especially you new people'?"

Heather nodded, as if considering the "Dana problem" for the first time. "Yeah, I guess she's a bit obnoxious." She then removed her sarong and stood, facing me, to row, pulling back, then forward, back, then forward.

It hadn't taken me long to realize that being aggressively naked as often as possible was what Lorna had meant when she said that Jeff's friends were really casual. I wasn't shy about peeing in the river in front of others, and I'd strip to bathe. But I couldn't understand why they wanted to lay bare all of themselves to a harsh, burning sun all the time. Maybe they thought they were being rebels. But it didn't look rebellious to me; it just looked strange and not all that appealing, on so many levels.

After a few days, we set up camp just above Tapeats Rapid to spend two days hiking the side canyons. I was relieved because, for one night, I would have access to my bag without Dana's begrudging say-so. The next morning, most of the crew went hiking. I stayed behind, thinking I'd have the camp to myself.

As I made my way to the coffee pot, I came across my new pal Buck's naked butt protruding from his tent. He had apparently tried to crawl in the previous night and hadn't quite made it all the way before passing out.

When the sun was fully up and beginning to burn Buck's butt, I woke him. He got up, shook himself off, and cracked open a warm beer. He spit out his first sip. "I need a cold one," he said, staggering over to his raft.

We found a slip of shade under an overhanging rock wall. After a while, Buck went to his boat and retrieved another beer for himself and one for me. We popped them open. *Cht! cht!* I no longer held any hope of this being a serene and transcendent trip down the Grand Canyon.

With a beer buzz on top of his hangover, Buck began firing his water gun at lizards scaling the rock wall. He eventually knocked one down and held it up to the side of his face, as if the lizard might want to kiss his cheek. Instead, it bit down on Buck's earlobe and held on. Buck swung his head, letting the lizard dangle like an earring.

Despite his bleeding earlobe, Buck wore that lizard until the rest of the group returned later that afternoon, naked, of course. They broke out appetizers. Jo-Bob leaned down to offer me some, with his "thing" swinging behind the plate of Vienna sausages.

The gang briefly clothed as a commercial trip approached in two motorized rafts. Families in bright orange life vests waved exuberantly at us. When the rafts nosed into the rapid below, roller-coaster screams of joy and fear echoed through the canyon.

"Commercial boaters!" scoffed Jo-Bob.

Connie smirked. "Tourists!"

Dana suffered another blow to her ego that afternoon when she came close to flipping in a small rapid. And that night, as we sat in the sand eating Hamburger Helper, she made another announcement: "I just want to make it clear, especially to any new people, that you have to wash your hands before cooking." Of course, I had cooked that night.

I should also add that Dana had suffered yet another blow to her ego earlier that day because she couldn't manage the entire hike and had to sit and wait for the others.

Emboldened by beer, I said, "What's this shit about 'especially you new people'?"

Dana placed her hands over her heart. "Oh, don't worry, we all love you. I just wanted to make sure everyone understood that it's important. I wasn't picking on you in particular."

Heather stood to get a second helping and said, "Yes, you were, Dana."

"I washed my hands," I said through clenched teeth.

Dana cocked her head and said sweetly, "Of course you did."

Later, Lorna approached me and asked if I was okay. I was so angry that just nodding my head made my eyes start to brim with tears. I walked off toward the boats clustered in the darkness, grabbed my face, and sobbed.

Toward the end of the trip, we camped above Lava Falls, the most notorious rapid in the canyon. The group seemed nervous. But Lava also meant the trip would soon be over, so I was in high spirits.

Around dusk, a wooden dory, fashioned after the boats of old, pulled into our campsite. Andy Hossman, a legendary Grand Canyon boatman, was at the oars, and he had two passengers. My first time down the Grand Canyon was on a dory trip with him as one of the boatmen. Dory rowers are the elite. They're old-school, and their boats are beautiful. Jo-Bob, Buck, and Jeff watched in awe as Hossman tied up.

I walked toward him, so happy to see a friendly face. He came up the bank, smiling at me, scarcely noticing our gawking group, and gave me a hug. He laughed and told me that because of some misunderstanding, he had missed their camp above us.

Jeff and Lorna told Hossman he could tie his boat there for the night. When he left to walk his clients up the bank to the dory camp, everyone in my group gazed at me with newfound reverence. Jo-Bob offered me a shot of his special tequila.

That night, Lorna said, "They're all impressed you know Andy. You're like a superstar now."

I said, "I'm touched." We both laughed.

The partying that night went on into the early morning. But somehow, they rallied, and we were up at dawn, rigging the rafts for Lava.

Jo-Bob and Connie went first, followed by Lorna and Jeff. Dana went next. Going into the tongue of Lava, she was too far right. As soon as Dana saw she was in trouble, she froze. The rapid slammed her into a lateral chop, and she fell out. The boat ricocheted back into the current, but waves pinned her against the rock while she struggled to keep her head above the water.

Being the next raft in line, Heather immediately pulled hard on the oars to move our boat toward Dana. "Get the throw rope!" she yelled to me as she put us on a collision course with the rock.

I held the throw rope in my right hand and the raft rope in my left to keep from sliding off the bucking raft. Just before hitting the rock, Heather pulled hard away, and I tossed the throw rope at Dana's big head. She grabbed it. The jolt on my right arm was intense, but I still had hold of the raft. The chill of the splashing fifty-degree water froze my breath and made it hard to drag Dana in. Heather pulled hard on the oars and got Dana off the rock. I used the surge of a wave to help pull her close.

"You have her?" Heather yelled, still plowing us through the rapid.

"Yeah!" I reached down, grabbed Dana's life vest by the shoulders, and heaved her up onto the bow.

She flopped into the boat like a big fish. Panting, she sputtered,

"Oh my God, I thought I was dead." Heather yelled, "Get the throw rope in!" I turned to the bow and started pulling in the rope.

"Thank you," Dana said. I looked back over my shoulder. "No problem," I said, trying not to bruise her ego.

THE PACK RAT

Apparently, the Creede Ridge fire started from a discarded cigarette. Nobody thought much of it. Still, some people pulled their cars over to look at the flames, and one or several exhaust pipes ignited the dry roadside grass, starting a second fire that spread rapidly. The vacuum between the two fires made way for a blowup, which ignited the valley.

My friend LuAnn and I were up in the Rio Grande Valley, cleaning cabins. We had been hired by the rustic Indian Creek Resort to ready the place for the fall hunting season. But when the fire blew up, it started heading toward LuAnn's house in Durango. We agreed that she should go home to evacuate while I tended to the resort.

I spent most of the days chopping wood, cleaning and mending cabins. During the actual hunting and fishing seasons at Indian Creek, cabin turnover had to be quick. But pre-season, a lot of attention had to be paid to all the accrued damage done by that year's flock of sportsmen, cigarette burns, fist-sized holes in the walls, congealed liquor, and "whatnot" stuck to the linoleum floors.

I was so busy during the days with work, I hadn't noticed the wind changing direction until ashes began falling on me. I looked around to see smoke billowing just beyond the lake. I debated clearing out and heading back to Durango, but after convincing LuAnn that it was okay for her to go, I figured I had to stay to fulfill our commitment to the cabin owners. Yes, that would be me, heroically standing tall against the raging forest fire to protect these small dwellings with a garden hose.

After a few days, when I still had not heard from LuAnn, I went to the office and discovered the phone was dead. I hurried to finish the chores as the fire encroached at an alarming rate. When I could see the flames, I figured the way out was compromised.

I moved my belongings to the fishing guide's hut at the edge of the lake. In case of a major blowup, I wanted quick access to water. The hut was small and basic, but I felt safe being at the lip of the lake.

I watched as the fire also pushed other creatures out of the thicket into the clearing. Moose plodded into the lake. They swam and grazed on the tall underwater grasses. When I swam, the moose would lift their heads up, water dribbling off their muzzles, and then go back to eating.

At dusk, as I sat out on the deck, a few coyotes would trot out of the forest. They didn't seem to mind me, nor I them, as they tumbled with each other and leapt after crickets. After four days of not talking to anyone, I walked around the lake to get closer to the coyotes, because I guess I thought I could establish some sort of *Dances with Wolves* connection. But they weren't interested.

One day, a big brown bear showed up at the lake. He scared off the moose and coyotes. I also retreated to the hut.

That night the air took on a considerable chill, and I made a fire. I spread a bag of frozen tater tots on a pan and opened the oven door. Crouched inside was a large pack rat glaring at me. Startled, I jumped back, scattering tater tots. I went to the living room, hoping the rat would politely show himself out while I tended the fire.

I grabbed a few pieces of wood from the neatly stacked pile in the corner. Heading to the fireplace, I paused, turned back to the woodpile, and saw the gray, hairy creature watching me. I left him alone and proceeded to the fire to stoke it.

Then I went to the bedroom to get a jacket. Opening the closet door, I looked down at the rat. *You've got to be kidding!* I thought.

The bed was just a foam mattress on the floor, so there was no way I was sleeping on it, not with that pack rat on the prowl. I was losing territory in the hut. Outside, there was a bear and a fire. I grabbed a blanket and trundled back to the living room to curl up on the couch with my book.

After a while, I looked over to see the rat lying curled in front of the fireplace. I thought, *That's it!* I stomped my foot to scare him off. The rat didn't budge, just gazed over at me. I considered its cuteness, cherubic cheeks and oversized ears, and harmless nature. I always believed that pack rats were basically benign collectors of shiny objects.

But this rat was taking over my turf, and his boldness gave me the creeps. I threw a matchbook at him. The rat sniffed the matchbook and settled back into his curl. I stomped my foot again. He didn't even bother to look at me.

For the rest of the night, I lay on the couch, half-awake, listening to an incessant clanking and scraping in the kitchen. Pack rats love pots and pans. Meanwhile, outside, it was beginning to snow, but still not enough high-mountain precipitation to put out the fire.

By morning, about an inch or two of snow covered the ground. Inside, in my cozy little kitchen, pots, pans, and cutlery lay strewn about the linoleum floor. Opening the oven door, I caught the rat wrestling with a metal rack. I slammed the door shut.

In the shed's loft, I found some Decon rat poison but opted for a live trap. I filled the metal wire crate with tater tots and went out to check on the forest fire. The spring snow was now coming down thickly. I could barely see the moose bedded down at the tree line across the lake. I went to the office.

The phones were still down, but the radio worked a little, so I scanned for news. Between bursts of static, I heard an announcer say that the fire was contained; it was no longer spreading. I figured this was my chance to get out. But first, I had to finish cleaning, which meant evicting a furry jerk of a rodent trying to claim "squatter's rights."

Returning to the hut, I heard a great deal of thrashing coming from the kitchen. *Yeah, buddy,* I thought, *it ain't so fun to be trapped.* When I got to the cage, I realized that the rat had attempted to escape by propelling himself through the grating. But only his head had made it through. His tater-tot-filled belly was stuck inside, his cheeky head stuck outside, as if in a guillotine. He was in proverbial limbo, and he didn't look so smug anymore.

I considered throwing the whole contraption into the lake. But seeing his head sticking out through the wires, I began to feel sorry for him. I rummaged through the cupboards and found a tin of Crisco. Putting on a pair of gardening gloves, I bent down and smeared lard all over the rat's head and neck. Then I palmed his head back through the wires.

The rat seemed sort of subdued as I portaged the cage a mile or so down the road for his exile. I let him out in some scrub oak. As he trotted off, he turned and gave me a look of gratitude, but no, wait, there was no gratitude there, just a surly look.

I went back to the cabin to begin packing. I planned to leave in the morning. I heated up a Lean Cuisine dinner and ate it with a glass of boxed wine. Then I retired to the bedroom. That night, the pack rat returned in my dreams, playing tin drums and making dramatic, repugnant facial expressions, as if he were in a punk band.

In the morning, I checked for the rat in the oven, the woodpile, and the bedroom closet. Satisfied that my visions were just a dream, I began packing up my car. After I finished, I went back in to shut down the cabin.

As I locked up, I heard a clanking noise. I peered in through the window and saw that damned, greasy-headed rat pushing a saucepan into his newly vacated bedroom.

Made in the USA
Las Vegas, NV
05 December 2025

35811047R10105